P9-CNI-456

Her fingertips brushed his, and their eyes locked.

And she felt a frisson of something magical go through her. Something hot and delicious and sticky like cayenne honey, flowing all the way through her veins.

And she could hardly breathe around it. She could hardly think. All she could do was stare. And feel the thundering rhythm of her heart, like a herd of wild mustangs, the kind that you could find out here in Eastern Oregon, and she was sure that he could hear it too.

And then, gradually, that didn't worry her. Because she could see in the look on his face that he was...hungry.

Hungry for her.

And she had to wonder if this was new, or if it had been there before.

Just like it was for her.

Maybe they felt the same.

She opened her mouth to say something, but then he lowered his head and kissed her.

A kiss had never scalded her like fire, searing her and leaving her feeling empty, a hollowed-out vessel forged by flame.

But his did.

* * *

Rancher's Forgotten Rival by Maisey Yates is part of The Carsons of Lone Rock series.

Select praise for
***New York Times* bestselling author**
Maisey Yates

"Her characters excel at defying the norms and providing readers with...an emotional investment."
—*RT Book Reviews* on *Claim Me, Cowboy* (Top Pick)

"A sassy, romantic and sexy story about two characters whose chemistry is off the charts."
—*RT Book Reviews* on *Smooth-Talking Cowboy* (Top Pick)

"This is an exceptional example of an opposites-attract romance with heartfelt writing and solid character development.... This is a must-read that will have you believing in love."
—*RT Book Reviews* on *Seduce Me, Cowboy* (Top Pick)

"Their relationship is displayed with a quick writing style full of double entendres, sexy sarcasm and enough passion to melt the mountain snow!"
—*RT Book Reviews* on *Hold Me, Cowboy* (Top Pick)

MAISEY YATES

RANCHER'S FORGOTTEN RIVAL

If you purchased this book without a cover you should be aware
that this book is stolen property. It was reported as "unsold and
destroyed" to the publisher, and neither the author nor the
publisher has received any payment for this "stripped book."

ISBN-13: 978-1-335-73540-9

Rancher's Forgotten Rival

Copyright © 2022 by Maisey Yates

Recycling programs
for this product may
not exist in your area.

All rights reserved. No part of this book may be used or reproduced in any
manner whatsoever without written permission except in the case of brief
quotations embodied in critical articles and reviews.

This is a work of fiction. Names, characters, places and incidents
are either the product of the author's imagination or are used fictitiously.
Any resemblance to actual persons, living or dead, businesses,
companies, events or locales is entirely coincidental.

This edition published by arrangement with Harlequin Books S.A.

For questions and comments about the quality of this book,
please contact us at CustomerService@Harlequin.com.

Harlequin Enterprises ULC
22 Adelaide St. West, 41st Floor
Toronto, Ontario M5H 4E3, Canada
www.Harlequin.com

Printed in U.S.A.

Books by Maisey Yates

The Carsons of Lone Rock

Rancher's Forgotten Rival

Gold Valley Vineyards

Rancher's Wild Secret
Claiming the Rancher's Heir
The Rancher's Wager
Rancher's Christmas Storm

Copper Ridge

Take Me, Cowboy
Hold Me, Cowboy
Seduce Me, Cowboy
Claim Me, Cowboy
Want Me, Cowboy
Need Me, Cowboy

For more books by Maisey Yates,
visit maiseyyates.com.

You can also find Maisey Yates on Facebook,
along with other Harlequin Desire authors,
at Facebook.com/harlequindesireauthors!

Legends of Lone Rock

The Sohappy family has its roots in Lone Rock. So deep that they precede the first European settler to come to North America. The ranch is part of their family heritage, passed on from generation to generation, from father to son.

The ranch has survived flood, famine and the perils of modern life.

In 1955, having no sons to pass the land to, Casper Sohappy passed the land on to his son-in-law. As family legend goes, the son-in-law did have roots, true and deep as the rest of the family. One night, he went out drinking at the local bar. The exact details of that night remain a mystery. But he woke up with a hangover, and a piece of paper indicating he'd lost the stretch of land between Sohappy Ranch and

Evergreen Ranch, granting essential water rights to the Carson family.

Since then the Sohappy families and Carson families have feuded.

And when the son-in-law passed on, his son vowed the land would never pass into the hands of someone who didn't carry their family's blood again.

He also vowed to see the Carsons pay for what they'd done.

And the hatred between the families began to go deeper than roots ever could.

One

Chance Carson couldn't complain about his life.

Well, he could. A man could always find a thing to complain about if he was of a mind. But Chance wasn't of that mind. Every day was a gift, in his opinion. The sun rose, the sun set, and he went to bed and woke up and did it all over again, and that was success no matter how it was measured.

Add in the fact that he got to work with his brothers, or take off and compete in the rodeo circuit as he saw fit, and he really did feel like he was living the dream.

And hell, he had to, right?

No one was guaranteed life.

Much less a dream. He knew well the tragedy of

a life cut short. It was a different grief to the death of an older person. It changed you. That unfairness.

He'd tried to at least take some good from those changes.

"You look smug," his brother Boone said from his position on his horse.

Five of the brothers were out, riding the range and looking for stragglers.

They had the biggest spread in Lone Rock, Oregon. Evergreen Ranch.

It had been in the family for generations, but had essentially been bare dirt until their dad had made his fortune in the rodeo, and further still as the commissioner of the Pro Rodeo Association. Now it was a thriving cattle ranch with luxury homes adding a touch of civility to the wildness of the surroundings. Courtesy of his family's status and success as rodeo royalty. They competed together, and they worked together. They practically lived together, given that most of them had housing on the ranch.

Though the rodeo hadn't always been a source of family togetherness.

Their sister, Callie, had nearly broken with the family over some of it, making inroads for women who wanted to ride saddle bronc, and now there was a blooming movement happening within the Association.

Chance was all for it.

Well, not as much when it concerned his little sister.

But in general.

He liked a little feminism. Who didn't?

Right now, they were off for the season, and hanging around the ranch, which was a bit more togetherness than they often got.

Flint, Jace, Kit, Boone and himself, all together like when they were kids.

Almost.

Sophie was gone, and there was no getting her back, a pain that he'd had to figure out how to live with. Grief was funny that way. People talked about "getting over it" and he didn't see it that way. It was just learning to live with it, learning where to carry the pain so you could still walk around breathing through it.

Then there was Buck. But his absence was his choice.

Being a prodigal in the Carson family—which was full to the brim with disreputable riffraff—was really something. But Buck had managed it.

But he was focusing on what he had, not what he didn't.

Which was good, since tomorrow he had to head out for a few days, just to see to a meeting with a man about buying another head of cattle.

"I *am* smug. It's another beautiful day in the neighborhood."

"If Mister Rogers were a cowboy…he wouldn't be you," Flint said. "You're an asshole."

"I'm not," Chance said. "I am the cheerfulest motherfucker out there."

"That's not a word."

"Your mom's not a word," Chance said.

"Your mom is *our* mom," Flint pointed out.

"Oh well. It stands. Anyway, I'm just enjoying the day. I'm heading out tomorrow, so I won't be around."

"Right. More cows," Jace said, and if he was trying to look excited about it, he was failing.

"It is what we do," he said.

"Sure," he said.

"You going to have time to come over to the bar tonight?" Jace asked. "Cara has some new beer she's trying out. She was wondering if we could all come taste it."

"I wouldn't mind having a taste of Cara's beer," Kit said.

And that earned him a steely glare from Jace. Cara was Jace's best friend, and it was not *like that*. And hell and damn to any man who wanted to be like that with her. Especially if he was one of Jace's brothers. Not, Chance imagined, because Jace was jealous, just because he knew how they all were. And that was shameless and not looking for a commitment.

"And where exactly are we putting the cattle?"

"You know where," Chance said.

"So, I was just wondering, because I was trying to figure out how long it would be before one of the Sohappy sisters was up in my face."

"Well, Boone," Chance said. "I think you know that Juniper and Shelby will be right at us like clockwork."

"It's like four feet of fence," Boone said.

"Doesn't matter. She thinks our great-great-granddad tricked hers into betting that land in a poker game while he was drunk and she lays into me about it every time we're near each other. And now it's been a fight for…oh, three generations, and our grandfather literally died mad about it." Not that their grandfather had been the most sterling guy, but it was the principle. "And I'm not moving the damn fence. And I'm not letting her badger me into signing something over to her just because of some tall tale that's been passed around the families."

"Well, yeah, because it's like four feet one way and like a mile the other," Kit pointed out. "Plus accusations of sabotage, cattle rustling and all manner of other bullshit."

"And I don't care if she has her panties in a twist about it, it's not my problem. If she wants to try and retroactively prove that her great-great-grandfather wasn't fit to sign over the land, that's on her, she's welcome to do it."

"She?" Boone asked. "I thought we were talking about both Sohappy sisters. Weird how it ended up being about the one."

And Chance wasn't at home to any of that. His brother liked to tease him that there was more than just rage between himself and Juniper. But no. Sure, she was beautiful. Both of the Sohappy sisters were beautiful. But ironically named, as far as he was concerned, because he had never seen them do much of anything other than scowl. At least, his direction.

Women loved Chance. He was a charmer. He loved women, so long as it stayed casual, and physical only.

But Shelby and Juniper Sohappy did not love him. And Juniper in particular.

Hell, yeah, Juniper was beautiful.

Long black hair, eyes the color of bitter chocolate, golden-brown skin, high cheekbones...

Shame about her personality.

She'd been a spiteful little scorpion since they were in school. And he didn't call her that to be hollowly mean; she'd once put a scorpion in his backpack when she was ten and he was twelve.

She'd hated him from the time his family had moved to the ranch when he was ten, taking over for his grandfather after his passing.

She'd hated him just because he was a Carson.

And hell, if he'd sometimes responded in kind to her provocations, who could blame him? And if he'd once bid on her at a charity auction and used her to do menial ranch tasks and carry his books at school—which she'd walked out on in the middle of, thanks—again, who could blame him?

Well, she could. And did. But that was beside the point.

And the fact that he'd do it again, even with all the sparks and spite it earned him, well, that was a whole other issue.

He liked sparring with her as much as he wanted to tell her to leave him the hell alone and never come back.

It was like a disease.

Like wanting to pull a girl's pigtails in second grade.

Except his other feelings about her were not remotely childish. Not at all.

"It's pretty bitter," Boone said. "Don't you think we should just get some surveillance done and see if that solves the issue?"

"Our grandfathers didn't. Our fathers didn't."

"Yeah," Boone said. "Grandpa also took cold showers because he thought that instant hot water bullshit made a man soft. I'm not sure 'because it's always been this way' is a good reason to do anything."

"You know," Chance said, "I would like at least one of them to ask nicely."

"And I would love to be standing there when you told her that," Flint said.

"Whatever. Juniper Sohappy and her bad attitude isn't my problem. She knows exactly what she can do if she wants to escalate it. But she isn't interested in that. She's just interested in being in a family feud that seems to always center squarely on me."

Because she could yell at any of his brothers. And never seemed to.

Almost as if she liked yelling at him.

Maybe *yelling* was an overstatement. When they'd run into each other at the market, in the cold beer fridge, each of them picking up some brews, she'd hissed. Like a feral weasel.

Gotta burr in your britches, Juniper?

Just a burr under my saddle. For life. That's you, Carson.

Yeah, I got that.

Flint shrugged. "All right, you may not want Juniper to be your problem, but I have a feeling she'll make it her goal to be."

Chance chuckled. "I'd like to see her try."

"Sure you would."

"You drinking later?" Boone asked.

"Nah. Gonna get an early night in so I can get on the road first thing."

They finished up their work, and his brothers trickled back home. And for some reason, Chance found himself riding toward the fence line, to the part of the property that bordered the Sohappy family's ranch.

It was just a shame, really.

A shame that he didn't see the rattlesnake. A shame that his horse chose to freak the hell out. A shame that his horse was a dirty deserter and ran off somewhere.

And it was a shame that when he fell, he hit his head directly on a rock.

It was raining. Of course it was raining.

Visibility was shit. Juniper had a feeling that she might end up taking calls tonight, whether she was supposed to or not. When the weather got like this, accidents happened. On these windy rural roads it was unavoidable. She wasn't supposed to be on shift tonight. She was supposed to be getting a good

night's sleep. She'd gone for twelve hours in a row
already.

Then there wasn't enough energy drinks in the
world to keep her going at this point.

Maybe she was just being grim.

But it was that damn Chance Carson. The Carsons in general were a pain in the butt, but Chance
specifically had gotten under her skin for years. She
was two years behind him in school, but it had been
enough for them to be in each other's paths quite a
bit, and every time they'd ever crossed…

It had been bad.

Then there was the general Carson-ness of it all.

Her parents told her that she was overreacting to
the whole border situation, but it mattered to *her*.

It mattered to her grandpa, who had hated the
Carsons for as long as she'd been alive, and had told
her stories of how they'd set out to undermine the
Sohappy family from the beginning. And most of
all how Chance's great-great-grandfather had gotten
her great-great-grandfather drunk, and conned him
into betting a portion of the ranch in a card game.

The legend went that he'd cheated. And he'd
taken a valuable piece of the Sohappy ranch away,
for nothing.

*Your father doesn't love the land, not like you do.
And I have no grandson. You're the firstborn of this
generation. The ranch is going to go to you.*

But Shelby is getting married. Shouldn't Chuck…

*You know what happened. When a man was
prized over blood. When the ranch passed from our*

direct line. It has to be you. You must care for it.
Nurture it like it was your child.

So she'd taken it on. Rearranged her ambitions.
It had been easy, actually. To put off pie-in-the-sky
dreams like medical school and pretend they'd never
really mattered.

The truth was, it had never been a particularly
attainable dream.

So she'd thrown herself into Lone Rock. Into the
ranch. Into life here. When she'd decided, at seven-
teen, that she'd stay, she'd rearranged every thought
she'd had about the future.

She'd let her roots go deep.

She was one of the ranchers down at the Thirsty
Mule, hanging with the guys and telling tall tales.
She'd earned that place. She could castrate calves
and move a herd with the best of them. And could
drink most of their sorry asses under the table.

She worked hard, she played hard and she didn't
accept double-standard bullshit.

What was good for the goose and all that.

She'd made a life she was proud of, and she'd
taken on the EMT job to pay the bills and satisfy
the medical itch she'd had when she was younger.

Now she'd educated herself on ways to expand
the ranch into something more lucrative.

A horse breeding and boarding facility. And
while she liked ranch work in general, horses were
her passion.

And if she got the facility going and got people

to pay for boarding, then she wouldn't have to work two jobs.

She was having to pay for ranching like it was her hobby, and the only thing that her family just had was this land.

Everything else was an expense. Everything else came out of all the hard work that she put in.

Her dad's soul just wasn't in the land the way it was hers. He cared, but he was devoted to his business, his career.

It was why Juniper had decided against pursuing medical school. Against leaving. Being a doctor was a calling, a vocation, and…

She wouldn't have been able to do both.

So she'd knuckled down and focused on what she could do. And now she was grateful she had. She'd figured out what to do with the ranch that excited her, made her happy.

And she was just fine. Just fine. And she didn't even want things to go differently.

Maybe don't think about that when you're angry and gritty and half-asleep.

Maybe. Yeah, maybe that was a good idea.

The dirt road that led up to her cabin was mud now, and she was feeling pretty annoyed. And when her headlights swept the area as she rounded the corner, she might have thought that her irritation and exhaustion played a role in what she saw.

It looked like a body. A body out there in the field.

Sprawled out flat. But it *couldn't* be. She slammed the brakes on in her truck and stared.

Yes. The rain was pouring down on what was very definitely a male form sprawled out there on the ground.

But why?

How?

She looked around for a second, evaluating the risk level of the situation, because if something had wounded or killed this man, she didn't want to be next.

She wasn't about to be the first fifteen minutes of a crime scene investigation show.

But she didn't see anything, and there were no points for sitting there wondering about it. Juniper got out of the truck and ran out to that spot in the field. And her heart hit her breastbone.

It was Chance.

Chance Carson.

She knelt down and felt for a pulse. She found one. Thank God. He drove her nuts, but she did not want him to die. At least, not on the border between Carson and Sohappy land. That would be unforgivably inconvenient.

She could call someone, but not here. There was no cell service right out in this spot in the ranch.

But she had her truck.

She rolled him onto his back and did a quick assessment for spinal injuries. None of that. But he was out cold. And what the hell was he doing out here anyway?

She couldn't tell what the hell had happened. But she had some medical equipment in her truck.

She ran back to the road, then pulled her truck out to the field, getting it as close as possible to him. He didn't rouse.

Shit.

She had a board in the back of her truck, and with great effort, she rolled him onto it, strapped him to it and used it to drag him over to the bed of the truck. He was strapped securely in like a mummy in a sarcophagus, so she propped the top up against the tailgate, then lifted up the end by his feet, and pushed him back into the bed of the truck.

"Sorry," she said, slamming the tailgate shut. Was she, though? She wasn't sure.

Well, she was sorry that he was hurt.

Her cabin was the closest place that she could get him dry, warm and examined. She was a medical professional, after all, and he certainly wasn't the first person with a head injury she'd ever dealt with.

The road to the cabin was bumpy, and she winced every time she hit a big pothole. She really didn't want to *kill* Chance Carson. He might think so, but not even she was that petty. At the end of the day, land was land, and it wasn't a human life.

It might feel like it was sometimes. It might feel like looking at this place was the same as opening a vein and letting all her hopes and dreams run red and free.

But it was land.

He was a human being.

Even if he was the human being who left her angrier, hotter, more stirred up and just plain trembly.

She hadn't realized quite how tense she was until her little cabin came into view, and then her shoulders relaxed immeasurably.

She just didn't like driving with him in the bed of the truck like that. It was unnerving.

She got as close to the front door as she could, and felt a little bit exhausted and sweaty staring at his inert form in the back of the truck, still on the board.

She could get him down there, to the front door, but it was just going to be a little bit of a trick. She eased her shoulders upward and rolled them, then grabbed the end of the board, doing her best to lower it gently down to the ground, getting him out much the same way as she had gotten him in. And then she… Well, she dragged him. Up the front steps, slowly, methodically, careful not to jostle him.

She got him into the front room of the house and looked around. Then she took all the cushions off the couch and laid them down on the floor. She unstrapped him from the gurney and rolled him onto the cushions.

He groaned.

Well, at least there was a sign of life.

His clothes were soaking wet, but she was not stripping him naked. No. She had lines, and they were definitely around stripping Chance Carson naked.

Her heart bumped up into her throat.

Well. Dreams weren't anything to get too worked up about. Granted, her grandmother would disagree.

But that didn't matter. Juniper didn't put any

stock in them. And the fact that she had dreamed a time or two about what it might be like to rip Chance Carson's clothes from his body at the end of an invigorating argument was… It was immaterial. She didn't think about it consciously. She didn't marinate on it or anything. It was her subconscious mixing up its passions. That was all.

She opened one of his eyes and shined a flashlight in it, then the other. "You are concussed," she said. "Sorry, my friend." She was going to have to observe him. Well, *someone* would.

She could take him down to the hospital…

Suddenly, a hard, masculine hand shot up and grabbed her around the wrist. "What's going on?"

His voice was rusty and hard. And she was…

On fire.

Her heart was racing, her skin suffused with heat. He had never…touched her before. In a panic, she pulled away and he released his hold, but the impression of his hand on her skin still remained.

"I…"

"Where am I?"

"You're at my house. I found you in a field. Can you tell me what happened?"

"I don't know what happened," he said.

"You don't know what happened?"

"That's what I said."

"Right. Okay. You don't know what happened."

"Yes," he said.

"That doesn't matter. It doesn't matter what happened. Can you see all right?" She put her finger off to his left, then his right, and watched as he tracked the movement. "That seems to be fine."

"Yeah," he agreed.

"No double vision?"

"No," he said.

"You definitely hit your head," she said.

"Right," he said.

"I'm just trying to figure out how serious it is."

"You a doctor?"

"No. I'm an EMT…" He knew that. Chance Carson knew that she was an EMT. Everybody did. "Do you know who I am?"

"No. Should I?"

Oh. Well. Holy crap. Chance Carson didn't know who she was.

"Juniper," she said slowly. "Juniper Sohappy."

"Name doesn't mean anything to me. Sorry."

"What's your name?"

His brow creased. "You know… I don't know."

He didn't know his name? Juniper couldn't wrap her head around that. He could be lying, of course. Though, to what end she didn't know, but how could you ever know with a Carson?

Wasn't her whole family history a testament to that?

If he was lying, she wasn't going to give him the satisfaction of tricking her. She…

She stopped herself just as she was about to open her mouth.

If he was lying, it might be funny to go along with it, see how long it took him to reveal himself.

And if he wasn't?

She thought back to the humiliation of when he'd had her working his land. Of every insult over the years, of everything.

She was going to keep an eye on him tonight, make sure he didn't lapse off and die of his head injury. And she was more than qualified to do it. She also knew if he really was suffering from some temporary memory loss from the fall he'd taken, it would resolve quickly enough and you weren't supposed to go heaping facts on people while their mind sorted things out.

What would it hurt if she taught him a little something in the meantime?

"You don't remember your name?" she pressed.

"No," he said, his eyes blank, and she looked hard to see if he was being genuine. "I don't remember anything."

Two

It was the damnedest thing, and he hadn't realized it until his pretty little rescuer had asked the question.

What's your name?

He didn't have a clue. Reflexively, he reached toward his back pocket, and felt that there was no wallet there. Which meant no ID.

Somehow he knew *that*.

"You can't remember," she pressed.

Her dark eyes were intense, and he couldn't quite get the read on them.

"No," he said.

But his head hurt like a son of a bitch. And apparently he knew enough to know that. But this wasn't normal, that he didn't like it.

"Chance," she said. "You don't know?"

"Chance," he said. "That's not a name."

"It is," she said. "Your name."

"Oh." He tried to see if it rang any bells, but it didn't. It didn't ring any at all.

Didn't bring to mind anything. There was just a big expanse of blankness.

"Well, you clearly know me. Who am I?"

"You… You work for me. You work here," she said.

He let that settle over him. "Okay."

"That doesn't ring any bells?"

"No," he said.

"You're… You're a cowboy," she said.

That felt right. It didn't ring bells, but it felt right. And apparently he worked on her ranch.

And he didn't know who this woman was, but she was the most beautiful thing he'd ever seen. Well, he didn't know all the things he'd seen. But he knew that. Somehow. Instantly. Electrically.

But it was more than beauty. It was deep.

He could swear he did know her, and that she mattered. That she was singular, significant. That she was the woman who occupied his thoughts, his fantasies.

"A ranch hand," he said.

"Well. Yes. But you know, you had such a hard time lately and… Anyway."

"A hard time?"

"I'd rather not tax you, Chance."

"You'd rather not…"

"You had a head injury," she said slowly.

"Yeah," he said. He rubbed the back of his head and felt dried blood.

"I don't think you need stitches," she said. "But it's pretty bad."

"Well. I don't have any context for that. Or if I've ever been… Hurt very bad before? How does this stuff work? Why can I remember… How to talk? But I can't remember who I am."

"Head injuries are complicated," she said. "That much I know. I can't say as I've ever run into anyone with amnesia…"

"It's not amnesia."

"I think it is."

And one thing he knew for certain right then and there was that he was not the kind of man who was used to being without his faculties. He wasn't the kind of man who wasn't used to being in control.

This was something he hadn't experienced before. And he didn't like it. Not in the least.

"I could drive you down to the hospital…"

"No," he said.

"No?"

"No. I don't want to move. I'm not… I'm not gonna die."

"No," she said. "And I have… Look, you definitely need someone to stay with you. You can't go back and sleep on your own."

Something fired in his blood, and he wondered then if… If there was something between him and Juniper.

Because it seemed fair to think there might be,

considering the way she got a response out of him even when he was in this poor of shape.

"I'll sit up with you," she said.

"Would I be alone otherwise?"

"Look, what you get up to with people is none of my business, but you don't live with anyone."

"Okay," he said.

So they weren't together. Had they been? Had he touched her? Kissed her? Held her naked in his arms?

The thought sent a surge of heat through him.

But he supposed it was just that she was his… His boss. That was strange, he didn't feel like he was the sort of man who had a boss. But he wondered if maybe he just wasn't the best judge of that sort of thing.

Maybe no man felt like he should have a boss deep down, but most people did. Because they had to.

"You should probably try to stay awake," she said.

"I'm so tired," he said. And that immediately felt… It was a strange thing, that admission. It was honest, but there was something about the admission of what was akin to vulnerability that didn't sit right with him. So whatever kind of man he was, he didn't truck with that sort of thing.

"I'll fix you some food," she said.

"Well, I don't want you to do that," he said.

"I need you to work it so that you are in a sitting position as soon as possible," she said. "You've got a concussion, and I don't want you dying on me."

"Can I help with anything?"

"No. I'm going to make you fry bread, and you need to stay away."

"If I've had it before, I can't remember."

"You probably have," she said. "But likely my mother's. Which is better than mine."

"I bet not." He didn't know why he said that. He just bet that he would rather have something made by Juniper than by… Maybe anybody else.

"I have dough ready to go." She took a bowl from the fridge and uncovered it, then took a large jug of oil from a cabinet beneath her stove, got a large pan and put a generous measure of the oil in it.

She waited, bustling around the room doing what appeared to be busywork to keep from having to look at him. He didn't know why he knew that, only that he did.

Then she took a small wooden cylinder from a container on the counter and retrieved dough balls from the bowl, rolling each of them out quickly, before dropping them into the hot oil.

Her movements were practiced and eased, whatever she said about her mother doing a better job. And as the smell filled the room, his stomach started to growl.

She put a wooden spoon into the pan and did something he couldn't see, then a couple of minutes later removed the dough, which was now golden and glistening.

She placed the bread in a stack on a plate and

put what looked like a heap of powdered sugar over the top.

"I'm not giving you alcohol," she said. "Not with a head injury."

"Well, I don't even know if I want alcohol." Except he found that he did. But he wondered if that was a good thing or not. Maybe he was one of those people who didn't drink in moderation. Maybe he had a problem. Maybe that was part of the troubles that she'd been talking about him having.

He didn't know, and he hadn't known for all of twenty minutes and it was starting to frustrate the hell out of him already.

There were too many unanswered questions in a moment. He had no idea what he was going to do if he eventually walked out of Juniper's cabin and found that he still didn't have any answers.

"Here," she said. "I'll give you a pop."

"A pop?"

She grinned. "A soda. My grandpa always called it that. So I do too. I don't actually know why. I think his wife was from the Midwest."

"You don't know for sure?"

"No, not about the crap on my dad's side. Because he had a few wives. On my mom's side, yes. My grandparents that are still here on the ranch have been together for sixty-five years."

"Hell," he said. "That's a long time."

"Yeah. I guess so. My mom's family has had this land for generations."

"Family ranch?"

"Yes. And it's very important to us." The sentence was heavy, and he couldn't quite say why.

"Do you work on the ranch, or just as an EMT?"

She laughed. "Just an EMT? I'll give you a pass because you just hit your head."

"That isn't what I meant. I meant… How do you find the time?"

"You make time to do what you need to. To do what you love. That's how it works. You do what needs to be done. At least, if you're worth anything."

"And you do what needs doing," he said. He had no trouble imagining it.

She brought a Coke and a plate of fry bread to where he was on the floor. "But you have to sit up," she said.

She reached out, and grabbed his hand, and helped him.

And maybe he should be embarrassed about that. But the only real thought he had was just how surprisingly soft her hands were, given that she was a woman who clearly worked hard. He had expected something different.

Surprising softness.

That was what he would remember.

Would he remember? Would he forget all this when everything else came back to him? He didn't know, and there was no way to know, so he just needed to quit thinking about it.

"How long have I worked here?"

Because what the hell else was there to do but ask questions about himself?

"A while," she said. "Eight months."

"Right. Where do I come from?"

She looked to the side. "Honestly, I don't really know. Sorry. You haven't shared a whole lot. I just know that you were going through a bit of a rough time. And we… Well, we've given you a lot to do, and focus on. Kind of a new start."

"That's nice of you."

"Yeah."

He didn't know why he needed a new start. And that was disconcerting as hell. Because that could mean a whole lot of things. He didn't know what kind of person he was. If he was a good one. If he was genuine in his appreciation for what this family had done for him, or if he was a con man. It was near impossible to know. And he didn't like that. Here she was, making him food—damned delicious food— and offering him beverages and to sit up with him all night, and he didn't even know what his intent was toward her. Or if he had any way of ever knowing.

"What about you?"

He wanted to know something. And if he couldn't know something concrete about himself, maybe he could learn something about the woman sitting across from him.

She looked confused, surprised. He wondered now if they'd ever talked before. If he'd ever asked her about herself. "Like I said, I'm an EMT."

"How did you get into that?"

A funny little smile crossed her face, the dimple to one side of her lip creasing her cheek. "My sister got hurt. When we were kids. We were playing out in the woods and she fell and she broke her leg. I wanted to be able to help her. I didn't know how, though. I didn't know how to help her, and that ate at me. I didn't know what to do to fix her. I asked my grandmother to teach me some things. Basic survival skills. She did, and I just got really into it. I thought maybe I'd…you know, go into medicine, be a doctor. But there's a need out here. I'm actually based out of the fire department. The rural fire department handles a lot of the medical emergencies. We're the first responders, until somebody can get here from the hospital. There isn't a hospital for forty miles."

"Wow," he said.

"Yeah. I don't know. I just like knowing how to fix things, more than I really wanted to help people, I guess." She laughed. "I mean, I like helping people, don't get me wrong. But my original motivation was… I wanted to be able to fix myself. Because, isolated like we are, we can't count on anyone else. It's like you and me right here. I can't call from my cabin. I don't have cell service. We would have to go down to the main house, and it's quite a drive. So… It just makes more sense for me to treat you here. And I know how."

"It's not serious?"

She laughed. "Well, I didn't think so until you didn't remember anything. I'm a little more concerned now. But as far as what I can tell? You're okay."

"What about the ranch?"

"It's been in my family for generations. It's… It's important to me. It isn't important to my dad, and it's the most important thing to my grandpa, and someone has to…carry the torch, I guess. That's me. My dad's a contractor. And the house that he's made for us there is amazing. And he makes enough money from it to support us. But he isn't interested in growing the actual ranch. He has his passion. And… The ranch is what my grandfather loves. He had horses. But that's all gone away now because he can't take care of things the way that he used to."

Conviction and passion rang in her voice, something that spoke to even deeper truths than she was admitting. It made him want to dig deep.

And he had no reason to question himself. Because he knew nothing. Why shouldn't he know everything about her?

"Does your grandfather still live on the ranch?"

"Yes. He and my grandmother still live in the original house. Not the grandfather that's had a lot of wives."

"I understand that."

"But… You know, there's this big family feud," she said.

"Family feud."

"Yeah. With us and… The neighbors. They're… They're dishonest is what they are. Crooks. They've been disputing the border of the land forever. But it's ours. In fact, years ago, all this land was ours. But my great-great-grandfather fell on hard times and he had to sell off a portion of it. And it just hits me wrong the Carsons are trying to take more. More than what we even had to get rid of back all those years ago."

She looked at him expectantly, as if she was very curious what he would say about that.

"Well, sounds like some bullshit to me. Why are they trying to take your land?"

"They're greedy," she said. "They never think they have enough. And it started with the great-great-grandfathers. When…when theirs took mine out drinking and got him to sign over a portion of the land that… It's very important. It sparked a major feud. Anyway. It's just important. And it's frustrating when something that matters so much to you is being badly used by a bunch of idiots who don't even really have ranching in their blood."

"They don't?"

Her lip curled. "They're showmen. Rodeo cowboys. My ancestors didn't believe in owning land. But the rules changed, and now we have to live by those rules. To have more taken from you is…"

"It's unconscionable," he said.

Land mattered. That he knew. That he felt in his blood, in his bones. With certainty. He didn't know why or how he felt it so deeply, only that he did.

It was real. That sense of ownership. It was real and it mattered.

"I've always thought so."

She sat down with him, and took a piece of bread from the platter.

"This is my favorite," she said, taking a bite. "My sister likes it with cinnamon sugar."

"I doubt you can go wrong," he said.

"Not in my opinion," she said. "My grandparents met in Arizona. This is my grandmother's family recipe. She moved out here to be with him when she was only eighteen. And her parents were furious. I can't imagine. She got married at eighteen. It seems almost ridiculous."

"Does it?"

She scrunched her face. "Don't you think?"

"I don't know. I don't know how I feel about marriage," he said.

Right now, he could see the benefit of it. You could hole up in a cozy cabin with a woman, she could cook you food and sit on the floor and talk to you. He didn't know anything except this moment with Juniper, and it felt like something important. It felt like something real. And he could imagine spending every day after this here.

That was probably the amnesia. Maybe. Maybe he was a commitment-minded man.

Maybe he was married. Maybe he had left a wife and children somewhere.

The idea was disconcerting.

"Maybe I should drive you down to the main house…"

"No," he said.

Something about expanding the scope of his reality didn't feel… It didn't feel right just now.

"Why not?"

"Honestly… I don't know. But the thing is, I don't know anything. I don't know anything, and the idea of jumping into… A lot doesn't sit well with me."

"Okay," she said slowly. "Then I'll sit with you."

Three

Juniper felt like a jerk. Well, it fluctuated. But right now she did. It was why she'd offered to at least take him down to her parents' place. Where they could tell her she was being awful and maybe help take control of this situation.

But he'd said no, and she was happy to back out. She knew why she'd let her own meanness goad her into this.

She'd been thinking about the time he'd bought her services in that high school auction and had made her work on his ranch. Mucking stalls and all things she was accustomed to, but working his land was anathema to her and he knew it.

And now she was sitting here cooking her grandmother's recipes for him, and in general sharing things with him she knew she shouldn't.

But he was still Chance.

And he'd been…well, unapologetically a jerk to her for the past twenty years, so what was so wrong with getting a little back while taking care of him?

Bottom line, she'd saved him.

And she really didn't think it was the right thing to do to explain everything to him. At least, she felt like she knew that from somewhere. She had given him his name, and she had talked about the Carsons, and nothing seemed to jog his memory. That concerned her, but so did the wild look in his eye when she had said that they ought to take him back to the main house. The fact of the matter was, she didn't know what had happened to him. He didn't know what had happened to him.

That thought made a shiver of disquiet race through her. Maybe there was danger out there. It was likely he had fallen off his horse…

But for all she knew, there was something else to it.

Anyway, there was no harm keeping him for the night. Keeping him settled here.

She really didn't think he was in any physical danger from his injury. If she did, she would've run him down to the hospital right away. But it just didn't seem likely. She knew enough about head injuries to evaluate him, and the fact that he was up and talking was a good sign. His speech was clear and coherent, and it wasn't slurred. His eye movement tracked, and they looked clear—no visible bleeds or anything. He seemed completely with it. Except for the whole *not remembering who he was*.

"Thank you," he said, taking another piece of bread.

And her heart did something weird.

Chance Carson had never been nice to her a day in her life. And now he was being... Well, he was being very nice.

And he looked disheveled and handsome, and she did wonder again if she should help him strip out of his wet clothes...

Probably not. Probably that was a really bad idea.

She needed to stop thinking of him out of his clothes.

She looked at him, and her heart did something very strange. And it was the heart reaction that really bothered her. Because a regrettable physical reaction to Chance wasn't completely unheard of. He was a good-looking man, and the fact that she noticed was inevitable to an extent. But she had to remember that he was her enemy. Her enemy. The Carsons were her enemy.

Fortified with that, she took a breath. And then took another piece of bread.

"Did you always know you wanted to stay here?" he asked.

And she wondered why he was asking her so many questions.

Maybe it was because he was trying to orient himself in a certain space and time. She could understand that.

What she really didn't know was why she was answering them.

"I... Yeah, I guess so. I've always been very close to my grandparents. And the land means everything to them. It's really hard to make a good living ranching. Especially if you don't have a lot of capital to invest to begin with. I want to move into hire and horse breeding. That's really where there's a shot of making some money."

"And money is important to you?"

He asked the question earnestly enough, there was nothing behind it. How could there be? He was a man who didn't remember anything. Just a big, beautiful log. He reminded her of Brendan Fraser in *George of the Jungle* right now.

That movie had been responsible for a certain level of awakening in her youth.

But she had never figured she'd meet a man who didn't understand the way the world worked, who was gorgeous and full-grown on top of it.

"It's not money so much as... Succeeding. Making my grandfather proud. I... I sacrificed some of my dreams and learned to make this my dream and I need it to matter." And she didn't know why she told him that. Hell, she could've made everything up, and he never would've known the difference. Even if he remembered everything, he wouldn't know the difference. She had known who Chance Carson was all of her life, but they did not know each other.

Amnesia or not, he wouldn't be able to pick her life story out of a lineup. So why she was telling him now, over her grandmother's recipe, she didn't know.

"Because your dad wasn't able to do it with the ranch?"

"I don't know that he wasn't able to do it. He just didn't care. But it's ours. It's our heritage. It's…"

"And that's important to you," he said.

"Yes," she said. But what lay beneath the surface of that affirmation was the fact that her grandfather was important to her.

The most important person in her life. And she just didn't know if she'd done enough to make him proud. She had done her best. To be the heir. The first girl to inherit the responsibility of working the land, of being the one in charge. She had plans and she wanted him to approve and to be proud and…

He was in his nineties. She didn't have limitless time.

"I just love him," she said.

"Your grandfather?"

She realized that she hadn't given any context for what she had just said, but that he had picked up on it anyway.

"Yes," she said. "My grandfather. I love him more than anything. I love him… He made me who I am. He taught me to ride. He taught me everything there is to know about this place. About what we can grow here. About what we can use that grows naturally. About how free you can feel out in the middle of nowhere with no one around to talk to. How you can just be. Just you. And the ground and the trees and the sky."

"What happened with your sister that made you want to be an EMT?"

She laughed. Entirely unexpected. "Yeah. Thank God for Shelby and her broken leg."

"Why not stay an EMT?"

"I won't have time. And anyway, eventually, the ranch should be self-supporting. It's not like I'm making a ton of money with what I'm doing. It's just enough. Enough to make sure that I'm supported. Enough to make sure I have some to invest in."

"And is this where you live?"

"Yes. All the time. Rent free. Which helps. Everything of mine goes back into the ranch. I have been fixing the same pair of boots for two years so that I don't have to fork out any money that I might need."

"That's commitment."

"Yeah, well. When it's your legacy, you just do."

She hadn't meant to spill all this to him. Honestly, she never would've talked to him under normal circumstances. She never would have spent any sincerity on him whatsoever. She yawned.

And he looked at her with… Concern.

"Are you going to be all right?"

"I'm going to keep you from dying."

"Wow. Nice of you. I don't think I'm going to die, though."

"I don't think you are either. Otherwise I would've forced your ass down to the hospital. I think we've got it under control."

She hoped she did.

"I don't want to go to the hospital," he said.

And it was a strange sort of fear in his eyes that made her want to listen.

She squinted. "Do you remember something about the hospital?"

He frowned. "I don't know. It just feels like a place I don't want to be. I don't know why. But look, I don't remember anything. I don't know if I'm a good man, I don't know if I'm a bad man. I don't know if I'm on the run from the law or from the Mafia. Or from a wife."

"Maybe you aren't on the run," she pointed out.

She'd planned to mess with him tonight, but she wasn't going to hold him here. In the morning, he really did need to go somewhere. But he might just remember. He might.

His expression went opaque. "I just feel like I might be."

She sat with that. Because she knew that Chance wasn't on the run. Not strictly. But it made her wonder. Because he seemed confident in a few things, not many, and she wondered if there was a grain of truth to them or if he was just drinking his bathwater. If amnesiacs didn't actually have any kind of sense of their former life.

"Well," she said. "I can only respect that."

"Thanks. Makes me feel like I might know something."

"Well, good. Unexpected silver linings." She had another piece of bread.

"What if we take turns sleeping?" he asked.

"That seems like a potentially dangerous idea."

"Or we set an alarm. You can check on me and make sure I'm not dead."

"Great."

She was tired, though. She had been exhausted when she pulled in at the end of the shift, and it was gone nearly one in the morning now.

At least her radio hadn't gone off. She didn't think he was severe. And as long as they kept on checking in…

"All right," she said. "Let me get some sleeping bags."

She went down the hall and retrieved two sleeping bags from her closet. She laid them out on the floor. He seemed more mobile now, but she was unbearably conscious of how cold he must be.

"I swear I'm not trying to get you naked," she said, wincing slightly. "But before we settle in, we need to get you out of these clothes."

It was the look on his face that got her. Charming and a little bit wicked all at once. As if he didn't mind one bit if what she was trying to do was get him naked, after all.

"You got a blanket for me?"

"Yes," she said. "Go to the back. To my room. Strip off, and I can get your clothes washed and dried."

"That's awfully nice of you."

"What's the point of saving you from a head injury if you die of hypothermia?"

"Well, that is a good point."

She went to the hall closet and grabbed a Pendleton blanket, big and woolly with bright geometric patterns on it, and flung it in his direction. "You can hunker down in this."

"Sure thing."

He went into her bedroom, and she paced for a moment. And when he came back out, he was holding the clothes and wrapped in the blanket, a disconcerting measure of masculine shoulder and chest revealed.

"Sorry I don't have any extra men's clothes." She migrated to the washer and dryer that were in the hallway. She chucked his clothes into the washer without examining them too closely. She didn't want to think about handling Chance Carson's underwear. Lord have mercy.

"I'm shocked you don't have an extra pair of men's jeans laying around somewhere."

"I'm not that kind of girl."

"Too proper to take a man home?"

"Too commitment phobic to let him keep a pair of jeans here. Or let him leave them behind. Once his ass is out of my bed, every trace of him better be gone, and if it's not, I'll just throw it in my burn pile."

It was true enough. The thing about taking on the mantle of being the heir to the ranch was that she had decided to go ahead and adopt all the perks that came along with it. She wasn't going to get married or have a family. She didn't care what anybody thought of her. She was going to behave the way the cowboys did. So when she wanted sex, she got it. She didn't do boyfriends. She didn't do relationships. She was a law unto herself, and that was how she liked it. Well, it could be argued that she was also a law unto her grandfather and her obligations to the ranch. And if they chafed a little more now than they had at one time…

The equine facility was the answer. It would give her a chance to show her grandfather that her own unique spin on things was right. It would give her a chance to keep her promise and then some. And it would fulfill her. The thing was, her grandfather had always been supportive of her. He was judgmental about a whole host of other people, so she knew what was involved in disappointing him. And she never wanted to do it. But she had promised him that she could do this. That she could be the thing that his own son hadn't been able to be, and she had liked that. That she had basically moved into being his favorite because she had made this vow.

And then she had discovered how difficult it was going to be to keep. The older she got, the more she questioned whether or not this was all there was to her life on the ranch. So change was the answer. Putting a stamp on it that was uniquely hers was the answer.

But then she got distracted by his shoulders and she forgot why she was thinking about her grandfather at all.

"I respect that," he said.

"You don't remember anything. How would you know not to respect it?"

He laughed. "I guess that's a good point. But I have the feeling that I'm a man who scratches an itch when the need takes him."

They looked at each other, and their eyes caught and held. And it was just a little bit too hot. She looked away, her heart pounding fast.

"Well."

"You got a deck of playing cards?"

"Are you kidding me? I have a tablet and a streaming service, we can just watch a movie."

"No way. You've already gotten the pants off me, we might as well play a rousing round of Go Fish."

"Wow."

She went back to her closet and rummaged until she came up with an unopened pack of playing cards. She tossed them to him, and he undid the cellophane on the outside, then pulled the cards out, shuffling them with ease and skill.

"You know how to shuffle cards," she said.

"Apparently. And I know how to play Go Fish."

"That's weird," she said.

"You're telling me."

He dealt the cards, and she sat across from him. And of course when he held his own cards up the blanket fell, down to his waist, revealing his whole chest.

Good grief.

If she had been told that she would be sitting with a bare-ass-naked Chance Carson in her house someday, she would have told whoever said that that they were crazy, and then gone to her room and cried because it would've made her hotter than she would have ever liked to admit.

That was the problem. Chance had always made her hotter than she wanted to admit.

He soundly destroyed her at the game, which piqued her temper, and she realized she had to keep it in check because he didn't know that they were rivals, not when it came to anything, so being generally persnickety regarding her loss had to have limits on it.

But by the time he beat her in round three, she chucked her cards at him. "I think you're cheating."

"Why would you think that?"

And he looked wicked, his blue eyes twinkling, his smile suggesting that he had never cheated at anything in his life. And he was a man who had the ability to tell himself that, because he had no memories.

No baggage. What a gift that was for a man like him, she bet.

"You're feral," he said.

"I am not."

"A little bit."

"Not."

"Come get your cards now, you gone and thrown a fit."

The cards were sitting in his lap. And he didn't think that she'd get them. Which meant that she absolutely had to.

She licked her lips, then she reached across the space, and somewhere along the way, she forgot exactly what her motivation was. If it was to prove her mettle, or if it was to be seductive.

She wouldn't say that seductive was normally in her wheelhouse. She was a woman who took a straightforward approach to sex. Because it just made sense.

It was easy enough. There was no fuss or muss required. She never felt the need to dress up or try to be anything she wasn't. But she bit her lip, looking up at him. And then slowly swiped a card from his lap. And the fire in his eyes leaped.

And she scrambled. She grabbed the remaining cards and fell back, realizing that she was overplaying her hand, no pun intended.

"Maybe Go Fish should be done now."

"I'm pretty tuckered out," he said.

"Well, let me put your clothes in the dryer."

"I don't mind sleeping nude," he said, shrugging.

Her face went hot—like she was some inexperienced virgin, and she went to transfer his clothes to the dryer, and by the time she got back, he was in the sleeping bag. In her sleeping bag, bare-ass naked. And she thought, just for a moment, about what it would be like to join him.

"We better hit the hay," she said. And she got down into her own sleeping bag. "You sleep first. I'll watch something with headphones. I'll set a timer and wake you up and make sure that you're all right."

"I feel well taken care of," he said, grinning at her.

He was so unbothered by all of it. And it turned out that, with or without memories, that was the thing that bothered her about Chance Carson the most.

He made her extremely bothered. And she wasn't sure that she could ever do the same to him in equal measure. Then she reached out and touched his forehead. "Just checking," she whispered. His jaw went hard, his blue eyes hot. And she could well imagine what was going on down in that sleeping bag. And just like that, she felt much better. Because maybe, just maybe, he was a lot more bothered by her than she thought.

And why exactly did you feel the need to prove that?

Why exactly anything. It didn't matter, though, because in the morning, all would be well. She could send him packing on back to his ranch, and forget that this ever happened. Forget that they had ever sat across from each other playing cards while he was naked. Forget that she had ever given in to the impulse to flirt.

Forget that she had ever let herself fully acknowledge the attraction that she felt to Chance Carson.

Yeah. In the morning, everything would be fine.

Four

When he woke up the next morning, he opened his eyes and felt a sense of urgency. And it took a full thirty seconds for him to realize he had no idea what the urgency was directed at. Because he didn't know who he was.

Chance.

The name echoed in his mind as he went and got yesterday's clothes out of the dryer and pulled them on.

His name was Chance, but it didn't really tell him anything that that was his name. Except that his parents had some weird tastes in names. He closed his eyes again and tried to picture… Anything. But all he could see was the liquid dark eyes of the woman who had taken care of him last night. The woman who had fed him.

Watched over him.

And when he opened his eyes and looked to his right, there she was. Her dark hair had fallen into her face, and her beautiful features were obscured. But that didn't mean there wasn't plenty to look at. He stood, and he felt dizzy, and his head hurt like a son of a bitch. But he supposed amnesia was never going to be painless.

Not that he ever had occasion to think about it before. He didn't think. He couldn't actually be sure. Since he couldn't be sure about any damn thing.

But he knew this place. He knew this woman. And he held on to that as tightly as possible.

He was a ranch hand. He walked toward the door and opened it, looked out the cabin, stunned by the view directly in front of him. The little cabin seemed to be built into the side of a mountain. Overlooking a vast and beautiful view below. The pine trees grew up tall and proud, and the patchwork of bright and dark green mountains seemed to stretch on endlessly. He could see notes of desert out before them too, flat, rocky outcroppings and deposits of porous-looking lava rock.

And it felt… It felt curiously like home. He had to wonder if he was from here originally, or if it was just that he had gotten accustomed to this place. If this was just the place he had decided to settle. But it felt too deeply ingrained to be anything quite so transient as a recent move.

It felt like something else. Something more. He took a step down the porch, and closer to the edge of the mountain, taking in a deep breath.

There was something about the air in his lungs that felt right. It felt right. In ways that he could never fathom. In ways that he could never explain.

Then he started to look around. For something to do. For anything to do. Maybe if he got back to the task at hand, any task, he would feel more like himself. He didn't know why but he had the sense that he wasn't idle. That he wasn't the kind of man to sit around and let grass grow beneath his feet.

He had a feeling that he had chosen a life of manual labor. That it was something that appealed to him. That it was something that made him feel centered. And since he couldn't really be one with himself at the moment, he would take being one with his surroundings. He would take anything, really.

He saw a stack of wood, all logs, big old rounds, and there was an ax out there.

He could chop wood. For some reason, he had no concerns about whether or not he could chop wood. And before he could put any thought to it, his body went into action. He set one log up longways on top of a larger one, then picked up the ax.

He split it with one fluid motion.

It was easy. The motion fluid, and he was right. There was something about it that made him feel accomplished. That made him feel like he was himself. Even if he couldn't remember anything, even if he didn't know who that was, or practically what it meant, he was himself. He was himself and that mattered.

So he started burning through those logs, as quickly as he could, till his shoulders and chest, the back of his arms, burned like hell.

Until he could hardly breathe, but he was getting a big old pile built up the side of him. And he didn't know why, but he had a feeling that if… If someone could see him, they would be making fun of him. For being extreme. For… For whatever thing it was that was in him that made him like this. Because this was him. He knew that. It was the weirdest thing. Like a word being on the tip of his tongue and him not quite being able to figure out what it was.

"Hey."

He looked up and saw Juniper standing there. She was wearing the same clothes from the night before, her dark hair a wild tangle. She made him ache. Not to know more about his life beyond this place. She made him ache to stay here. "What are you doing?"

"Cutting wood," he said.

"Do you think it's a good idea to be up cutting wood?"

"You're the EMT. I'm sure you can tell me whether or not it's a good idea."

"I don't think so," she said. "Hey…"

"It made me feel better," he said, cutting her off. "It did?"

"Yes. It made me feel a little bit more like myself, whatever that is. In fact, whatever chores you have."

"Look," she said. "I need to take you somewhere.

Your memory still hasn't come back and it made sense for you to be here last night, but going forward…"

"No," he said. "Do you know what anybody does about amnesia?"

She looked down. "As far as I know, they wait for it to resolve."

"Then let's wait for it to resolve. Here. I want to wait for it to resolve here." She looked hesitant. "Look," he said. "I don't know any details about myself. But I just know that I don't want to leave here. I don't know why. But it might be important."

"Chance," she said, her tone firm. "I'm not a doctor. I'm an EMT and you…"

"I don't want to," he said, his tone hard.

He didn't know why he was so certain he needed to be here. That he needed to be with her. The world was one entire lesson he had to learn, but for some reason, this place—she—felt like the one he had to learn first.

And he might have no real basis for that conviction, but it was strong and clear and real.

"Do you have jobs for me to do? Can I be useful here?"

She hesitated. "Oh. Oh. Well. Yes," she said. "The wood. Thank you. And… Well, I've been working on restoring one of the barns."

"You have been?"

"Yeah," she said.

"Well, let me come help with that."

"Chance…"

"I am a man who knows what he wants," he said.

"Even if I'm not a man who knows who he is. And I don't think I take kindly to being told what to do."

She sighed. "No. But right now what you are is a very confident man with no memory."

"I have the feeling that I'm very confident," he said.

And she bit her lip as if she wanted to say something. Yet again, he wondered at the actual details of her relationship to him. He had a response to her that seemed to be bigger than just boss-employee. But then, it could be that he had been attracted to her already, and it was just that it was exacerbated by the fact that now he couldn't remember their roles.

"I have to get ready," she said. "You will probably also need a change of clothes."

"Yeah," he said. "That is true."

He didn't want to leave here, though. Didn't want to go to his home, or lean-to, or whatever it might be. She seemed to realize that.

"Why don't you go in and have a shower?"

"Sure."

"I'll… I'll be back with whatever you need."

Juniper was cursing herself all the way down to Shelby's place. And she knew that she would be cursing herself even more once Shelby heard what she wanted, because she was going to be pissed off at her.

Chance wanted to stay. And it was one thing to haul his dead weight, but quite another to think about forcing his big, muscular frame—*oh dam-*

mit, Juniper, can you not objectify the man even in this?—out her front door if he didn't want to go.

But what if his family worried? Granted, there were lots of Carsons and they seemed to come and go as they pleased, and she had no idea how often they all communicated.

But Chance didn't have a phone or wallet or anything on him.

You could just tell him the truth...

No, she couldn't. It could harm him. Like waking a sleepwalker.

Also, he'd know you were a liar and all the nice things that happened last night would disappear.

That wasn't the problem.

It was the cognitive issues. That was it.

"Hey," she said when she rolled up to the door.

Shelby had chin-length hair, and rounder eyes than Juniper. She also had grooves by her mouth from frowning. She was younger, but life had really worn itself into her face. Juniper doubted it had been avoidable. Shelby had had a rough couple of years. And a better moisturizer would hardly have kept the evidence of her pain away.

"Can I come in?"

"Why?"

Juniper smiled brightly. "Can't I just come visit my sister in the morning?"

"You can," Shelby said, narrowing her eyes. "You *don't.*"

"I need to borrow some clothes."

"I am four inches shorter than you, Juniper."

She felt bad now, her heart squeezing. "No. I need to borrow some of Chuck's clothes." She softened her voice when she spoke of her former brother-in-law.

"Oh," Shelby said, her expression going blank for just a moment before she suddenly brightened. "Why? You got some dude naked up at your place?"

Juniper rolled her eyes. "Well. Yes."

"And he needs clothes?" Shelby smirked. "Are you a *quitter*?"

She couldn't help but laugh. Because of course her sister would take it there. "I have stuff to do. I can't lounge around naked all day."

"I wasn't suggesting lounging, J."

"I'm *aware*," Juniper said.

"Why doesn't he have a change of clothes?"

Juniper let out an exasperated sigh. "Look. It's complicated. Just indulge me. Just give me something for a man to wear."

"All right." Shelby stepped away from the door and let Juniper into the small, cozy house. It wasn't as old as her cabin, which had been built in the 1920s. This was straight out of the '70s with wood paneling and shag carpeting. It was the house they'd spent part of their childhood in, until their dad had built the sprawling, modern home their parents lived in now.

Even if it was a little dated, Juniper would always find it warm and lovely. Homey. She wondered how Shelby felt now, though. It was supposed to be her home. Her family home, and now…

Well, *now*.

Shelby led them back to her room, and suddenly, Juniper felt strangely uncomfortable.

Everything in there was untouched. Just as it had been. And Chuck's clothes were still in the closet.

"You know, you don't have to loan me anything if…"

"I need to get rid of it," she said. "It doesn't matter whether they're hanging here or not. He's gone. He's not going to come back. I'm not going to have a séance with his favorite flannel and get him to come say *hey* from the beyond."

"I know. But if you want to keep his clothes and not have another man in them…"

"It's you. It's not me. If it were me having a sexual partner who needed some clothes, that would be weird. And I would not do that." The very fact that her room was exactly as it had been, with her wedding picture on the nightstand and a closet full of his clothes, told her that there wasn't any chance of that, since there were no men coming over anyway.

"I just… I don't know when I'd be able to get these back and…"

"I'll just give you a pair of black jeans and a black shirt. I couldn't tell you the difference between those anyway. They're all the damn same. The man had no fashion sense."

He had also been quite a bit shorter than Chance, but Juniper wasn't going to say anything. Beggars couldn't be choosers, and anyway, she wasn't bringing up the fact that it was Chance Carson who needed the clothes. All the better to let her sister think that she had picked up a guy for an uncharacteristic one-nighter.

"You're not fucking around with Jamie, are you?" she asked.

"What?" The lovely blond man that she often worked shifts with had a boyfriend. But clearly her sister didn't know that.

"You were on shift last night," Shelby pointed out.

"Right," she said. "No, look, it's not like that. It's not… No. Not Jamie. Whatever. Don't worry about it."

"I can't help it. I do worry about you. You're my only sister. And you've been… Very moody lately."

"I am not moody," she said.

"Yeah, you are," Shelby said. "You're a moody beast."

"Hey, you're the baby. I'm the one that's supposed to worry about you. Anyway, you're the prime example of stability?"

"No." Shelby shrugged. "But I have an excuse."

"Sure. Play the grief card." Gallows humor was really the only way to cope. At least, the only way Juniper and Shelby had found.

"Glaaaaadly," Shelby said, drawing the word out and finishing it with a smile. "I have to get some benefit out of this."

She didn't think the clothes would be a great fit for Chance.

Not that she was an expert on his body. Not that

she had been looking. A lot. Since she was thirteen years old.

No.

Well. She *wished* that were true. She wished that she were wholly and totally immune to Chance and his looks.

And really, she wished that she were immune to the god-awful pettiness that had made her decide she was going to play this game with him.

But there's a point to it.

Maybe there was. Maybe there really was. Maybe it was possible for him to begin to understand just why all of this was so important to her.

Maybe he could understand why the land was so important to them. Maybe without all the baggage from his own family, all of the ridiculousness, and the ridiculous male ego nonsense that had been entrenched in him over the course of their feud… That was it. It was that there was so much nonsense between them.

So much.

And maybe with all of this there would be less.

He'd seemed…human last night. And that made her feel something shift in her chest. She didn't like it.

Except, of course, when he remembered and… No. She wasn't going to think about that. He would've gotten to know her maybe a little bit and by then she would be… Humanized or something.

"What is that look on your face?" Shelby asked.

"What look?"

Her lips curved upward. "Your visitor must've been something else in the sack."

She shifted uncomfortably. "Why do you say that?"

"Because you are *spacey*."

Juniper snorted. "I don't get spacey over men."

That was true. She'd had a few boyfriends, but they hadn't been serious. And she hadn't been heartbroken when the relationship had ended. Hadn't missed them in her life or her bed.

Sex… It didn't matter that much to her. She had other things to worry about. Other things to focus on.

Her sister had been *so* in love with Chuck. He had been her one and only.

And she had acted sort of interested in the idea that Juniper had been able to have more than one partner.

But Juniper didn't see sex as anything more than a basic itch that occasionally needed scratching. And she had found often that it wasn't really all that scratched when all was said and done.

All to build up a little fanfare.

Minimal fireworks.

She didn't really know how to pretend that there had been epic fireworks.

Though, apparently, the distraction level caused by Chance was something that her sister imagined might be fireworks. Well, in fairness, it wasn't Chance himself that she found so distracting. It was the fact that she was lying to him. And that he had amnesia.

Yeah. That.

"Thanks."

"Want to have a coffee?" Shelby asked.

"I should… Get back. With clothes."

Shelby looked a little disappointed and Juniper went ahead and threw that disappointment right onto her guilt pile.

But Chance was *without spare clothing in her house* and that had to be solved.

"Right. Okay."

She scurried back out, got into her truck and began to drive back to the cabin.

And when she scampered into the house, she did so just as the bathroom door was opening, and Chance came out in nothing but a towel.

Juniper's jaw practically hit the floor. Maybe if any of the men that she'd been with had looked like this…

His body was unreal. She'd noticed that last night. Well. She'd noticed it a long time ago. But it still took her breath away. Broad shoulders, well-defined muscular chest, narrow waist with abs her grandmother could have grated cheese on for enchiladas.

All covered in dark hair that made her fingers itch with the desire to test the texture. The desire to touch them.

"Sorry," he said. "I didn't mean to ambush you."

He was *glistening*.

It was, like, not even fair.

"It's fine," she said. She took a step toward him

and handed him the clothes, feeling like she could straight up sense the heat coming off of his body.

He disappeared into the bathroom, and she sat there, unbearably aware of her heart pounding in her ears.

When he reappeared, it was in black jeans that were two inches too short.

"Thank God for boots," he said.

"Sorry," she said. "They were my… They were my brother-in-law's. He wasn't as tall as you."

"Wasn't?"

Dammit. She hadn't meant to bring all this up.

"My brother-in-law, Chuck, died in a car accident a couple of years ago. My poor sister… She was devastated. She loved him. I mean." She rolled her eyes at herself. This was never easy to talk about, and it wasn't getting easier. "Obviously she loved her husband. It's just they were childhood sweethearts. It was deeper than it is for a lot of people. He was the only one for her."

"That's sad," he said. He didn't say anything for a long time. "Kind of amazing, to have the one for you. Even if just for a little bit."

She stared at him, and she didn't know if he was like this all the time, or if this was something to do with having all the… The *Chance* wiped away.

But maybe the Chance was there. Maybe she just didn't know him.

This is supposed to be making him like you, not the other way around.

She cleared her throat. "Yeah. I mean… I don't

think she would've traded it for anything. It's just really sad."

"Of course it is."

She shook her head. "I mean, I know it sounds really dumb. But it is."

"You're an EMT," he said.

She nodded.

"Were you called to the scene of the accident?"

That he'd connected those two things, and then gone ahead and asked the hard question… It made her chest hurt. Made it hard to breathe.

She took a breath. "I… Yes. Jamie, my partner. He… He recognized Chuck. He knew. He told me not to come any closer. I was desperate to, but he said… Chuck was already gone. He spared me from the worst of it. I'm thankful." She tried to swallow, her whole body seizing up. Sometimes she was angry that she'd had to do it. Sometimes she was grateful. She could never decide which. "But I will never be over having to tell Shelby."

"Has that impacted your relationship?"

"If anything, it brought us closer. I was there for her during the hardest night of her life. I had to give her the worst news. Nobody should have to tell their sister that. And yet… Who else but your sister should tell you? Who else but your sister should be there to hold you?"

"That's an amazing perspective," he said.

"Maybe. We didn't have a choice. So we just make the best out of it. You ready?"

"Yep."

Without speaking, they walked out of the house and to her truck.

When they were closed inside the vehicle, she realized she had made another error. She hadn't fully considered what it would be like to be closed in the space with him. Hadn't fully considered the way he might smell. Or what it would feel like to be in such close proximity to him.

Her breathing became more rapid. And she felt like an idiot. Like a straight-up idiot.

And now she was basically hyperventilating. Her heart was going a thousand miles a minute, her senses were... Swamped with him.

He had used her soap. He had no other options. And it was just a generic bar brand, and it smelled so good coming off of his skin.

Like there was some magical Chance additive that had gone into it. It was him. His skin. The pheromones.

She wouldn't say she had wondered. What it would be like. If when they were done fighting they just... Fell into each other. If they tore each other's clothes off, and finished it that way. On the ground. On the floor of her cabin. Nowhere in her fantasies had they ever managed to make it to a bed. No, she and Chance Carson would never make it to a bed. They were destined to be against the wall, on the floor...

Nowhere, idiot.

Nowhere. They would never have sex anywhere.

He had never shown any indication that he might want to.

Ever. And that was good. It was good.

"The barn is up here," she said, because she had to distract herself.

Good God, she had to distract herself.

"What kind of work are you doing?"

"Well, I've been reroofing."

"Reroofing?"

"Yeah," she said.

"By yourself?"

"Partly. I mean, mostly."

"Was I helping you with this?"

"No. We've mostly been… We have some cows. Not that many. And some horses, which is what I'm building up. And you mostly help with that kind of thing. Cows are mostly your thing."

The thing was, she didn't have any idea what Chance knew how to fix or anything. So she had to make sure that her lie was something he already knew how to do. Which was cattle ranching. She had a feeling he'd have the muscle memory for that. Not that she would actually let him get down to get anywhere near the cows. No. That was not going to be a thing.

"Well, I'm pretty confident I can swing a hammer as well as I can swing an ax."

"I appreciate it."

They pulled up to the old barn, and she suddenly felt self-conscious. It was nothing like the kind of barn that would be on the Carson spread. Where everything was new and perfectly kept. But then, he didn't remember that. So maybe he wouldn't judge hers quite so harshly.

He surveyed the place, and she watched his expression closely. "There's a lot of work to be done," he said.

"I know," she said.

"Don't take it personal," he said.

"About taking it personal. It's just that I have done a lot of work."

"I'm sure you have."

They got out of the truck, and she felt irrationally annoyed, and that made it feel a lot more like the Chance that she knew. It helped temper the attraction. That was the problem. He hadn't been annoying. So the way that she felt when he was around hadn't defused the fact that she wanted to punch him in his ridiculously handsome face. And now all was well. All was right with the world.

She understood herself when she wanted to punch Chance Carson in the face.

Maybe that was sad. But she didn't much care.

It was fair. It was more than fair.

She went over to the base of the ladder and picked up some tools. "Let's go," she said.

"All right," he replied.

He began to climb up the ladder ahead of her, hammer gripped in his hand. She suddenly worried about having him up there. And she wondered if she was being a little bit cavalier about his safety.

But physically, he seemed just fine. Everything

seemed to be in fair working order, and it seemed as if he was capable of ladder climbing.

She came up behind him and found herself staring directly at his ass. It wasn't the first time she had looked at Chance's ass. But it was the first time she'd had such a prime view.

"You checking me out back there?"

Her head snapped up. "What?"

That had sounded more like Chance. Cocky. Exceptionally male.

"Are you checking me out?"

"I'm thinking about roof tile," she said.

"Sure," he said.

He looked back behind him, and he winked. The bastard winked.

She felt tetchy. But at least she wasn't mired in the sadness of a few moments earlier.

But then he got up onto the roof and was towering above her, and she scrambled up behind him, standing up as quickly as she could so she wasn't kneeling at his feet.

That was a bit on the nose.

"We got the nail guns all ready to go," she said. "So…"

"Let's get to it, I guess."

And he did. Making her own time on the roofing look sad.

"So you know how to do this," she said.

"I guess so. It's like the wood," he said. "I didn't know for sure if I'd ever done it before, but my body knew how to do it. So, I guess there are just some things that are like that." He looked up, and his eyes caught hers and held.

And she couldn't help but think of all the other things a person's body might actually remember how to do.

Oh. She didn't need to be thinking about that right now.

Remember how he's your sworn enemy, and you're just looking at his ass?

Yeah. She was sort of a disgrace, all things considered.

"Sorry about your brother-in-law," he said, between nails.

"Me too."

"You married?" he asked.

She huffed. "Have you seen a husband around?"

"No."

She really didn't need to be playing this brand of getting-to-know-you with Chance. And yet… She couldn't resist him.

"Ever been married?" he asked.

"Nope. Not even close."

"Why not?"

She shrugged. "Don't see the point of it. I think it's kind of bullshit, actually. I mean for me. Not for everybody else. My parents are in love. My grandparents are in love. My sister was really in love."

"So why is it bullshit?"

"It's just not for me. I don't think that I have the capacity for it. I don't know. I've never been all that worked up about any of the men I've hooked up with.

Anyway, it doesn't work. Not doing what I want to do. A man can get a wife, I guess, to run his house while he works the land. I have to figure out how to do it all, and I've never met a person I wanted to try to fit into all that. On top of that, I just don't see how it would work practically." She swallowed hard. "I wouldn't respect a man who didn't have the drive I did. I couldn't be with a man who didn't have land. If he has his own land, he won't be coming to live on mine. And I certainly won't leave."

"A man ain't no kind of man unless he has land? I feel like I've heard that somewhere."

Of course, Chance didn't think he had land. But he did. A lot of it.

And that's your fault that he doesn't know, because you're a lying liar.

Yes, she was a lying liar. She felt kinda bad.

But not enough to *quit* lying.

Not enough to...

Not have him. Not have this anymore.

"Something like that."

"But?"

"If I was with a man who had the kind of ambition I did, if I was with a man who had land, then what would we do with mine? I just don't think things can work that way. Shelby and Chuck built their lives around each other. It wasn't about a ranch, or a career, for either of them. It was just about this life that they wanted to share. Everything was about each other. For my parents, it was about my dad. His business. My mom wanted to be a homemaker, and that was what she loved. She took care of us, she does beadwork, and just kind of works around all of her household duties. It's not anything she was ever ambitious with. My grandmother is kind of an extreme homemaker. She did everything joyfully, but busily. Always working. My grandfather was that way with the ranch. They share the homestead. And they were contributing toward it. If she had been doing that in one place, while he had been doing it with another, it would not work."

"And you wouldn't be happy with your horses on a different plot of land."

"No. I couldn't be. That's the thing. This is Sohappy land. And that means something to me. The heritage of it means something to me. I decided to pour myself into this at the expense of everything. I could never… I could never walk away from it."

"So, because of all that, you can't find a man who brings out strong feelings in you."

"Basically. I think that's the problem. I just… I'm not built for it."

"I wish I could tell you my story," he said. "The reasons that I think love and marriage are bullshit. But I don't even know if I think that."

"You probably do," she said. "Men who look like you…"

"Look like me?"

"Did you get a chance to look in the mirror?" she asked.

"Yeah," he said, lifting a shoulder.

"So you must know you're good-looking," she said. "I mean…" She waved her arm up and down.

"Thanks," he said. "I guess I didn't really think about it."

"Well, there's no point beating around the bush."

He laughed. "I guess not. You think I'm trouble?"

"I *know* you're trouble," she said.

And his eyes met hers again, and it felt hot and weighty, and she didn't like it.

"Just better keep moving before it gets warm," he said.

"It's funny," she said, letting herself become distracted. "It's funny the things you know."

"Yeah. I guess it is. Still don't know anything about myself." And she could feel him staring at her, long and hard, and she didn't look back. "I feel like there's something there," he said. "Between us."

Oh, that was so dangerous. And it made breathing nearly impossible, and she hated him for it as much as she wanted to launch herself into his arms.

That, at least, was normal.

But she wondered…treacherously, she wondered… if that meant that without all the anger, without all the memories, without everything…

If he felt this.

If he had.

"You work for me," she said.

"Right."

And then they let that subject drop.

They worked until the heat of the day was too much, then they climbed down. Juniper went to the bed of the truck and took out a cooler, where she had packed a couple of boiled eggs and ham sandwiches.

"I don't know if you like ham," she said, handing him a sandwich.

"Neither do I," he responded. He took a bite of the sandwich. "I do," he said. "I'm hungry as hell."

She realized that one sandwich probably wasn't going to be enough for him.

"You can have my boiled egg," she said.

A paltry offer, really. One egg. But all things considered, she owed it to him.

The lying being considered?

"Awfully nice of you."

"Well," she said dryly. "You don't know anything about me, but I am *very nice*. That's what people say about me."

"Why do I get the feeling that's not strictly true?"

She shrugged. "I don't know. Not my fault if people are sometimes incorrect."

"I don't know much, really. Literally. But I sense that a lot of people are not as observational as they should be."

"I would agree. People get entrenched in their own ways. Their own beliefs, and they never really look at anyone else. They never look around. And never challenge themselves."

She was speaking of him, of course. Him and his outrageous prejudice against her. Him and his certainty that his ancestors were being truthful about who owned that section of land.

But she felt it. She felt it resonated in her own heart. In her own chest.

And she hated that.

This was all supposed to be about him. About getting him to see things in a new way, about getting him to respect her and her family.

It wasn't supposed to change her.

"Now we get to go inside and replace the floorboards."

"Sounds like a party."

Inside, there were planks that she had precut the other day with her skill saw. They were measured out ready to go, they just needed to be nailed in.

"Fun with power tools," he commented.

She huffed a laugh.

And what was really strange was that she was having fun with him. That spending the afternoon with him was better than spending it alone.

It's not him, though.

And she would do well to remember that.

"Have I met your grandfather?" he asked, out of the blue.

"Yes," she answered truthfully.

"Does he like me?"

Well. She wasn't sure if she should answer that truthfully.

"You're taking an awfully long time. I'm wondering if I'm not going to like the answer."

"He doesn't like very many people. Or rather, I should say he's not impressed with very many people."

That was true. Her grandfather was as crotchety as they came, and he had opinions. Big opinions about who was good, who was worthy of respect and whether or not he had to pay it to them.

She liked that about him.

He was a curmudgeon. He didn't let anyone know he had a soft spot, right at the center of his soul, that he reserved for the sky, the river and the land itself. That he was a man who loved the earth he'd walked on all his life more than most people loved anything.

He might not show his feelings, but he had them.

And it was so important to her—so very important— that she honored the trust that hard, stubborn old man had put in her.

He'd bypassed his son as the heir to the ranch.

He'd bypassed his son-in-law.

His belief was in her and it had been clear and bright from the beginning. And she'd taken the reins and promised to ride hard and true.

It was only now that sometimes…

Sometimes she wondered if she could love this ranch and this ranch alone.

Too late now.

"He doesn't have much use for you," she said. "But… That is actually true of most people. And my grandfather… He loves his family. He loves his dogs. He loves his land. Otherwise… Well, his feelings aren't all that strong."

He laughed. "I can respect that. As long as he's good to you. And recognizes how wonderful it is to have earned your admiration. I have a feeling a man could spend his whole life trying to get that, Juniper."

"Really," she said, her throat suddenly feeling dry. "What makes you think that?"

"You just seem like the kind of woman that doesn't impress easily. I like that about you. You seem like you're a whole thing."

"I am."

It was sweaty work, but they finished the flooring, and her stomach was growling ridiculously by the time they finished.

"I'm starving," he said.

"Luckily," she said, "I have some meals my grandmother made me in the freezer. I'll just heat up a double portion."

"I will never say no to a grandmother's cooking. Another thing I know deep in my soul."

"Great."

"And what are we getting tonight?"

"Stew. And bread. It's wonderful. She makes her own sourdough."

"And you don't cook?"

"No." And then she felt a kick of sadness inside of her heart, because she didn't cook because her grandmother did. Shelby did, thankfully, but she did sometimes wonder where the recipes would go when Grandma was gone.

"It's amazing that she still bakes," she said softly. "She's ninety, and she hasn't slowed down. But I worry. I worry it won't be long before she does. That's just life, isn't it?"

Maybe that was the problem lately. Time was marching on relentlessly. Chuck was gone and it marched on. Her grandparents were getting older and older and it marched on.

She was…just her. Just here.

And it marched on.

"I don't have a lot of specific memories about how life is," he said slowly. "But it seems to me that life really is like that."

Her chest got tight. "I guess I should ask for her recipes. But part of me doesn't want to. Because sometimes I think maybe when she's gone we don't deserve to have her food anymore. We should feel the absence there too."

"But it's heritage, right? Like the land."

"Like the land," she agreed.

They got in the truck and drove back to her cabin. And she was thankful that she hadn't run into anyone from her family. They didn't often come out this far, but it wasn't unreasonable to think that they might come to bring her some food at midday. It happened occasionally.

Her mom might not bake quite like her grandmother, but she would often bring bologna and mustard, or some chocolate chip cookies.

She didn't want to explain why she had Chance Carson working with her. And why Chance Carson didn't know who he was. And why Chance Carson thought they were maybe friends, and that he was an employee of the ranch.

No. She really didn't want to get into all that.

"It's a nice evening," he said.

"Yeah," she agreed.

"I notice you have a firepit out there. You want to eat dinner outside?"

And… She found that she did. She wanted to sit with him by the fire, and she wasn't even certain why.

"Yeah. In fact, maybe I'll get out the Dutch oven and heat the stew over the fire."

"Sounds great."

He'd said that to her more than once today.

Sounds great.

And it did funny things to her chest. Because Chance had never said that anything sounded great to her before. She might have said it to him, but that could've been when he asked if she would see something over his dead body.

Sounds great.

Except, when she had found what she thought might be his dead body, she hadn't done a dance or anything like that. In fact, she had helped him.

That made her feel a little better about her eternal soul. Sometimes she had wondered.

He got the fire going. Another one of those things he remembered, apparently. And she got the big Dutch oven, and the frozen block of stew, and got it set on a grate over the firepit.

There were little camp chairs that she set by the fire ring, and she brought out a couple of beers and handed one to him.

It didn't take long for the stew to start bubbling,

and then she ladled it into tin camping bowls, and they sat and ate.

"Is this elk?" he asked.

She frowned. "Yes. How did you know that?"

"I've had it before. I mean, I just know. I don't know. I guess it's something I've had before."

"Obviously," she said. "Common out this way."

"Right."

"My dad is a big bow hunter. So we always have meat. I imagine that…" She almost said she imagined his dad was too. In fact, she was sure of it. But she shouldn't go saying things like that. Not when she was doing her best not to give him details about anything. Because it was the right thing to do, really. For the handling of the amnesia. But also she didn't need to go implicating herself in anything.

"I imagine you would've had it before." That finish was lame. And she knew it. But if he was suspicious, he didn't say anything. She stared into the fire, and then over the flames at him.

Dusk had begun to fall, and stars were punching their way through the curtain of blue velvet above, and as it darkened, they grew stronger. The light shining all the clearer for the darkness around it.

"It's a beautiful night," she said.

"Yeah. Such a strange time of year," he said. "Beautiful. But there's something sad. In these hours just before darkness. When it's warm still but the sun has gone away. I don't know why."

She stared at him, like she'd never seen him before, and she knew that he wouldn't even find it all that weird. He didn't know that she had seen him most days for a good portion of her life. Whether it was catching a glimpse of him across the Thirsty Mule on a crowded Saturday night, or in the grocery store, or when she saw him, silhouetted by the sun, riding across Carson land.

Those moments when she wanted to hate him but felt something else instead.

"But you just know that?"

He seemed to be wrestling with it. Or concentrating hard, like it was a feat to hang on to it.

"It's a feeling. It's a feeling that I have as strong as anything."

"I see. Well... I guess maybe it's long nights?"

He shook his head and stared past her for a while. And she had the feeling when he spoke again, he wasn't speaking to her, but using words as a way to write this truth on his heart. So he wouldn't lose it. "It's something more than that. I can see a little girl. A little girl and... She's not mine. Because I'm a little boy. She's very sick."

"Oh."

"That's why I don't want to go to the doctor." He sounded far away then. "She went to the doctor all the time. Hospitals. So many hospitals. All the time. A never-ending rotation of them. When she died, it was late spring like this. One of these long nights."

The sounds around them were amplified. The flames licking over the wood, cracking. The crickets, insistent, rhythmic, somewhere in the darkness.

"Who was it?"

She didn't know. This was a story about the Carson family she didn't know.

"I don't know. I just know that I see her. And that when you asked me if I wanted to go to the hospital, I thought no. That's where people go to die. And she's why I think that. Because she was a little girl, and one day she went into the hospital and she never came out."

An overwhelming, heavy sadness pervaded Juniper's chest.

"You know, I take people to the hospital every day," she said. "They don't just go there to die. They go there to be healed. I understand that there can be bad traumatic memories connected to that. But... But the hospital can be a good thing."

"Logically I know that. But..."

"I'm sorry," she said. "I'm sorry that the first memory you're having is so sad."

"I think it's probably the strongest one I have. Because I think I felt that sadness inside of me before I ever saw her face. What a hell of a thing. That I almost died. Out there in the field. When..."

"When what?" she whispered.

"My parents have been through enough," he said. "She must've been my sister."

"Oh." The word left her body in a gust.

He knew what it was like to lose someone. He was...human.

Just the same as she was.

Just the same as they all were.

The Carsons and Sohappys weren't so different.

She was hoping he might see that during this time, but she hadn't expected it would be her own lesson.

She…she had never heard anything about that and she didn't know why he thought it. Or if it was true. And it still settled hard in her chest.

He was getting way too close to remembering things, and it was getting… Dicey. It was one thing to think that she wanted to endear herself to him this way, but him sharing something personal like this, something he never would've shared otherwise, it felt like a violation. And she had never thought that she would feel like she violated Chance Carson. But this was different. The situation with his sister.

No. He had a sister. And she was alive and well.

Callie Carson was much younger than him, and she had gone off and married a rodeo cowboy who lived in Gold Valley.

But the way he was talking about it, it sounded like he was younger.

She felt hungry for more, but at the same time she didn't want to press him. For so many reasons, but maybe the biggest one was her heart felt so tender right now. For him.

That wasn't supposed to happen.

"All right," he said.

He stood up, and she stood at the same time, ready to take his bowl from him.

"I can take the dishes."

"Oh no, that's okay," he said, and she put her

hand on the bowl, and her fingertips brushed his, and their eyes locked.

And she felt a frisson of something magical go through her. Something hot and delicious and sticky like cayenne honey, flowing all the way through her veins.

And she could hardly breathe around it. She could hardly think. All she could do was stare. And feel the thundering rhythm of her heart, like a herd of wild mustangs, the kind that you could find out here in Eastern Oregon, and she was sure that he could hear it too.

And then, gradually, that didn't worry her. Because she could see in the look on his face that he was… Hungry.

Hungry for her.

And she had to wonder if this was new, or if it had been there before.

Just like it was for her.

Maybe they felt the same.

She'd always thought she and Chance Carson felt absolutely different. About everything. But maybe not.

Maybe they felt the same.

Maybe they always had.

She opened her mouth to say something, but then he lowered his head and kissed her.

It was like an electric shock. His mouth was hot and firm, his lips certain and miraculous as they moved against hers.

She clung to him, instinctively, and it wasn't until

she heard the bowl clatter to the ground that she realized she had let go of the metal vessel. And she was glad it wasn't glass.

But it was a metaphor. A metaphor for how precarious this was. Because she was forgetting. And she was letting herself get caught up in all the wrong things.

But she couldn't help but be caught up now. In his hold, in the searing kiss, the magical pressure of his mouth on hers. She'd had any number of kisses. But they had just been something to do.

Because when you thought a man was attractive, you might as well kiss him. Because even though it wasn't like she had gone to bed with that many men, she had never found it to be that big of a deal, and if she was in a relationship, she was all right taking it to its natural conclusion.

A kiss had never scalded her like fire, searing her and leaving her feeling empty, a hollowed-out vessel forged by flame.

But his did.

She was so hot. Everywhere. And she ached. Not just between her legs, but in her chest. It hurt how badly she wanted to be close to him.

How much she wanted to tear away their clothing that stood between them, how much she wanted to press herself flush against him with nothing between them.

She had never wanted like this. This quickly. This violently.

It was a sickness.

But it was a beautiful one.

She clung to his shirt, then pushed her fingers through his hair, arching against him, rubbing her breasts against his solid chest like a cat.

He growled, and then rolled his hips forward, and she could feel the insistence of that hard length between them.

On the floor. Against the wall.

She had thought about this.

And she wanted him. But… He didn't know who she was.

He didn't know who he was.

She jerked away. Horrified. And she realized that she was snared in a net entirely of her own making.

"I'm sorry," she said. "I'm sorry. You work for me and…"

"But that's not all there is between us, is there?" he asked, his voice going husky.

No. Of course it wasn't all there was between them.

Of course it wasn't.

But she couldn't say that. She couldn't explain. Anyway, the explanation didn't make things any clearer. The explanation was even more confusing. He wasn't her employee. And they weren't having a secret assignation.

They were enemies. Caught between a family feud, and nothing more. Two people who had driven each other nuts for an age. Not anything deeper than that. How could they be?

"It's just… I'm sorry. It's not right. It's not right."

"I'm a man," he said. "And I know that. For certain. Whether or not I have all my memories. I know how to cut wood. I know how to fix a roof. I know how to put in a floor. I think I can figure out how to…"

"That's not what I'm worried about. I am worried about taking advantage of you."

As she stood there with her head coming up to the middle of his chest, she realized that what she was saying sounded ridiculous. But she understood.

Way to go, Juniper. Caught in the net of your own idiocy.

"I'm sorry I…"

"It's all right," he said. "Look, I can leave if you want. I don't need to stay here. I can go back to my own cabin if it…"

"No. I'm fine. I don't… It's not you. I promise."

"I'm not going to hurt you," he said.

"I know that," she said. "I trust that. You have never… You've never given me any indication that you would. No matter… No matter what. Even if we were fighting."

"All right." He nodded slowly. "As long as you trust that."

"I do."

Five

Sleeping on the living room floor in Juniper's place was more uncomfortable tonight than it had been the other night. Because he was hard as a rock and unlikely to find sleep. But he had meant what he'd said to her. He wouldn't make any advances on her. No matter what. Not if she wasn't interested.

It was hilarious, her being worried about his consent. He had made his pretty clear. But then, she had concerns about his memory. Or whatever.

Even if we were fighting.

That word came flooding back to him.

Fighting? Had they fought? The way she said that made it sound like they had. Sometime.

And he couldn't help but wonder why. What about.

She had acted like she only vaguely knew him, but he was starting to get the impression that wasn't true.

He was up before the sunrise and set about fixing coffee and eggs.

Juniper woke up not long after, dressed in utilitarian gear, clearly ready for her shift as an EMT.

He found her fascinating. And beautiful.

"I'll see you later," she said. "I have to work. I… I'll bring you back some more clothes."

"Sure," he said.

"Sorry you just had the one spare outfit. Sorry about… Everything."

"None of it's your fault."

"How are you feeling about staying here?" she asked.

"It's still what I want," he said. "If you don't mind."

"No," she said. "Not at all. If this is where you want to be, then… Great. I… I'm happy to have you."

"Hey, can I head over to the barn and do some finish work for you today?"

"Sure," she said.

"I'd like to keep helping out. I'd like to make myself useful in my invalid state."

"I appreciate it. You don't need to do that."

"But I enjoy it," he said.

And that was that.

He left the cabin and went out walking. There wasn't a vehicle left up at her cabin, so it was up to him to make it there on foot, but he didn't mind. He remembered the route to get down there, and it was a pleasant walk.

The stormy weather of a few days ago had vanished now. Spring flowers making themselves known, dots of yellow and orange in a brilliant field of green.

His mind was pleasantly empty. And right now, it felt pleasant. It was strange, how he knew that this was different, even though he couldn't quite remember what it was like to have his mind be full. Last night had maybe been a preview of that. He had been so preoccupied thinking about the things that had happened with Juniper, that thing that was niggling at him that she'd said, that he hadn't fully marinated on that memory from his childhood. The little girl. His sister. He was sure. Even though he didn't know her name. Even though he didn't really know his own name—not beyond what Juniper had told him—he felt a sense of certainty over the images there. In the feelings they created. He had been a child. There was something different about his eyes and those memories. And there was something about the pain in his chest. The way that it bruised. As if it was a fresh betrayal brought on by life. Not just another of life's bullshit moves.

No, this had been something unique. Something special. The pain that was the first of its kind. Back when the world seemed bright and full of possibility, this had been his first indicator that things could go terribly, horribly wrong.

It had shaped him, this pain. It had changed him. There was a before, and there was an after.

Even without his memories, he was still living in the after.

But he chose to focus on the day around him, and not on those memories, and he wondered if that was what he did. If he was the kind of man who didn't dwell on hurt, if he was the kind of man who simply walked forward.

He walked across the field and made his way over to the barn. He climbed the ladder, ready to do the work now. He began to nail more tiles into the roof surface, and right as he was finishing one section, he stood, and his boot heel wrapped around the edge of the cord. He pitched forward, and he saw the ground far below rising up to meet him. But he didn't fall. He caught himself. But still, it took him back to a moment, and suddenly, he could see another fall in his head.

He had fallen off the horse. His horse. He had fallen off of his horse and hit his head on the ground. While he had been riding the line between Carson land and Sohappy land.

Carson land.

He had been on Carson land, because he was a Carson.

And Juniper Sohappy was his rival.

By the time Juniper pulled into her sister's property, she was exhausted. She had stopped at the Thirsty Mule and had picked up burgers to go, and had had a difficult time making eye contact with Cara Thompson, who was Jace Carson's best friend, so even though she would never be outright rude to Juniper while she was in the woman's place of business, she didn't like Juniper, and she didn't do a very good job of hiding that fact.

If only she knew. If only she knew that Juniper had Chance squirreled away up at her cabin, and Chance didn't know who he was.

She had worried about his family and their concern for him before, but now that she knew about their loss, it…

It ate at her.

As soon as Juniper closed the door to her truck, her sister's front door flung open, and her sister came bounding outside. "What the hell?"

"What?"

"I saw Chance Carson up on the roof of your barn today, wearing Chuck's clothing. And so you have to answer my question."

"I do not guarantee that I will answer your question," Juniper said, her mouth going dry.

"Are you going to pound town with Chance Carson?"

"Don't say *pound town*," Juniper said, practically covering her ears.

"Doing the horizontal Macarena?"

"Stop it."

"Screwing. Are you *screwing* him?"

"I am… I am not *screwing* Chance Carson."

Of course, the truth was so ridiculous she should probably stick with the story that she was…banging the man, because her sister was never going to believe that Chance Carson had amnesia, and that she had lied to him, and they were currently doing a modern-day dramatic reenactment of *Overboard* with him as Goldie Hawn to her Kurt Russell.

No. That wouldn't go over very well at all.

But she had to try and explain. Somehow.

"He…" She scrunched her face. "He got hurt."

"He got hurt?"

"Yes."

"Why was he naked at your house?" she pressed.

"He wasn't naked at my house specifically. I mean, he has been. You know, when he was showering or changing his clothes. Not *with me*. But he fell. Off of his horse or something, the details are fuzzy. And I found him in the field unconscious. I took him back to the cabin because it was the middle of the night and we're so far away from the hospital, and I am a professional, so I looked at his head, and he had a concussion…"

"None of this explains what he is doing there, and why he is wearing my husband's clothes."

She hedged. "He can't remember anything."

"He can't *remember anything*?"

"No," she said. "Least of all that he hates me. I mean, that he hates all of us."

"Oh, Juniper."

"I might have… I might have a little bit told him that he's working for me."

"Do you have a death wish?" Shelby practically shrieked that question.

"No. I don't have a death wish. I don't wish to be dead at all."

Shelby's dark eyes were wide. "He's going to kill you."

"No, he isn't."

"When he finds out that you were lying to him, that you made him do menial tasks for you while he didn't remember who he was, he is going to *kill you*. Strangle you with his big, capable, roof-repairing hands."

"You are being a drama queen." But there was a thread of truth to her words that disquieted Juniper.

"I'm not being a drama queen, you're being a sociopath. And, I grant you, Juniper, I really admire the brand of crazy that you're being. Because this is petty on a level that I could never even aspire to. And I value pettiness. I value it with all of my being. I am so deeply impressed by this, but I worry for your safety. Because if you are by yourself when he finds out…" She suddenly stopped talking, and her eyes went wide. "But are you *sleeping with him, though*?"

"I'm *not* sleeping with him," she said.

"Not even a little?"

"How do you *a little* sleep with someone?"

Shelby huffed a laugh. "Oh please. You're the one who has had multiple sex partners."

"Don't say it like that!"

"More than me anyway, and I think you know exactly how you can a little bit sleep with someone. Are you sucking his…"

"No." She needed Shelby to not finish that sen-

tence. Badly. "I kissed him. Once. I told him that it couldn't happen again. Because I'm not actually a sociopath, Shelby, and I cannot sleep with a man who thinks that he works for me, when he is in fact my mortal enemy. I will screw with my mortal enemy all the livelong day, but I will not take advantage of him physically in that way."

"Well, thank God you have some scruples remaining in you. But this is deeply disconcerting."

"I don't know what to tell you. I just… It just happened, it tumbled out of my mouth. I was very tired, and then there was no going back."

"I don't even know what to say."

"Get me some clothes for him, or…"

"He's going to have to walk around the cabin naked."

Her face went flushed. She could feel it. "No," she said. "He will not be walking around naked."

But what a visual that was.

"I have deep concerns for your safety. You need to have your walkie-talkie on you at all times. When he finds out, and he literally tries to kill you."

"He isn't. He isn't going to try to kill me. He's… Look, the worst part is I kind of like Chance. I mean, Chance without his memories."

"It's *not* Chance," Shelby said insistently. "We're not who we are without our memories. If I didn't remember all the horrible shit that happened in my life over the last couple of years that…"

"It might be nicer?"

She sighed wearily. "It might be nicer. But I probably wouldn't be me. And the minute that he remembers, he will be him, and he's going to go back to being the person that he always was. This isn't really him. You have to remember that."

"I know. I promise you I'm not going to get hurt."

Shelby sighed. "Right." She said nothing for a moment. "But how good of a kisser is he?"

There was a keen sort of interest shining in Shelby's eyes and Juniper knew why. But they never talked about it. Ever. It was an unspoken law.

Never mention Kit Carson, or the way Shelby looked at him.

So she didn't. Even though she wanted to.

Juniper growled. "Just get me some clothes, please."

Shelby returned with a stack of clothes and handed it to her with a skeptical expression. Juniper snatched them close to her chest and looked at her sister's hopeful expression.

"He kisses like a dream," she relented.

"Oh, that is really good to know. The Carson men are… Well, they are problematic."

"Agreed."

"So are you," she said.

"Noted," Juniper shouted as she ran out of the house, ignoring her sister's further calls to not get murdered by Chance.

She got into her truck and drove back up to the cabin. And when she got there, Chance was standing in the doorway.

But it wasn't Chance, the man that she had spent the past several days with.

It was Chance Carson.

The *real* Chance Carson.

And he did in fact look like he might have murder on his mind.

Six

He could see the moment she registered what was going on. He could see the second she realized that she was looking at him. Really him, not the man that she had been playing around with for the past few days.

No.

She was well aware of who she was looking at in that moment, and he was fascinated. What would she do? How would she try to talk herself out of this? Would she? In his experience, Juniper was confrontational. A hellcat if ever there was one, and the little creature was more likely to bite than anything else.

He looked at her face, and he waited. Then she held up a bag that was in her hand and smiled. "I brought hamburgers."

Interesting. That's how she was going to play it. She was going to make him say it.

"I'm not in the mood for hamburgers," he said, crossing his arms and leaning against the post on the porch.

"That's too bad," she said, her grin somehow brightening. "I would've gotten you a salad if I would've known."

"I don't want a salad."

"Well. I guess there is some middle ground between a hamburger and a salad. But I didn't realize. I'm sorry."

"You know what I would like?" he said.

"What exactly?"

"I'd like an explanation."

Her eyes darted left, then right, and she put him in the mind of seeing her as a scared bull, trying to figure out which way to scurry.

There was no way to scurry. Not from him.

"Well, I finished my shift, I am quite tired, but I stopped at the Thirsty Mule anyway to grab some hamburgers from Cara. You don't know who Cara is, though." That smile became all the more determined.

"I don't?"

"Not as far as I know," she said, smiling sweetly back.

And that was the thing, the weirdest thing. What hit him then was that while he hadn't known who she was, she had known who he was the entire time. She had been well aware that he was Chance Carson, that they theoretically hated each other, and she had kissed him.

Enthusiastically.

Had pressed that tight little body up against him and practically begged for his touch. In fact… He had a feeling that if it hadn't been for his memory loss, she would've taken it all the way.

She had weird lines, did Juniper. Apparently, there was no issue lying to him and using him for manual labor, but she wasn't going to take advantage of him sexually.

He supposed he should be grateful for that. Not that he would've felt overly taken advantage of.

"Not as far as you know," he repeated. "You know, I've been thinking," he said.

"Have you?"

"Yes. I've been thinking about the kiss the other night."

"Oh."

"It was good."

"I… Yes." Her face was scarlet red, and he could see her doing the dance. He could see her uncertainty. Maybe she wasn't entirely sure if he remembered or not, and it was making her nervous. Making her uncomfortable. Good.

He took a step toward her. "I'm not in the mood for hamburgers. I'm in the mood for another kiss."

He knew that his voice had a dangerous edge, and he could see her respond to it. Could see her pupils widen, could see her breath get shallow. She was afraid of him, but she was also intrigued. She was aroused. Turned on, and more than a little bit interested by what was happening between them.

He felt a smile curve his lips, and he knew it wasn't a kind one.

"I told you it wasn't a good idea," she said.

"Right," he said. "You're so worried about taking advantage of me."

Rage thrummed through his veins as he advanced on her, as he moved to cup the back of her head with his hand.

Her hair was so soft. She was soft.

And he never would've thought that Juniper Sohappy was soft.

He'd've thought she would be like embracing a cactus. All prickles and spikes, and maybe hard steel underneath.

But no. She was a woman.

She smelled like honeysuckle and the warmth of the sun. She was impossibly beautiful. And he wanted her.

And dammit, he felt owed.

She had been screwing with him. Laughing her ass off having him do her chores while he couldn't remember anything.

All over a piece of land?

And he had told her things that… Things he didn't talk about. Because he didn't remember that he didn't talk about them.

It was a damn shame.

But nothing he couldn't correct by getting some of his own back.

He watched as her pulse fluttered wildly at the base of her throat.

She was a beautiful creature. He wanted to lick her there. Run his tongue along the smooth column of her neck.

And he realized right then that what he wanted more than anything, more than punishing her, more than making her pay, was to make her scream.

Beneath him. Above him. However she wanted it.

He had buried that. All these years he had buried that. He had acknowledged that she was beautiful, but he had never allowed himself to fully give in to the desire that arced between them every time they fought. But her kissing him back had proved that she felt the same, and it had opened the floodgates of his own need.

And honestly, the worse she was, the more of a little weasel she was, the more he wanted her. Angry and hard and complicated.

Chance didn't do angry, he didn't do hard, he didn't do complicated.

Chance liked a bar hookup with a pretty, easy girl who didn't have any connections to his actual life. Chance liked a woman who was there for a good time, not a long time. He liked to keep it easy. Because he didn't like complications. Because complications meant entanglements, and entanglements meant attachments, and attachments were just something he wasn't willing to do.

For all the reasons he remembered now. Deeply. Keenly.

"Don't you want to kiss me again just a little bit?"

"No. I was being stupid. I was being crazy. And I…"

He closed the distance between them, kissing her hard.

And there was no way that she wouldn't be able to read the difference between this and the previous kiss. Because they were nothing alike. In this kiss, he poured all of his frustration. All of his rage that she had tapped into something emotional inside of him that he preferred to never acknowledge. Into this kiss, he put every ounce of withheld desire. All of the need that he had chosen to shove down deep for all of these years. Because he couldn't sleep with Juniper. She was the bane of his existence. She was…

She was the damned sexiest woman he had ever held in his arms, and his body felt like it was on fire.

He had never been so angry at a woman in his entire life, and at the same time he was utterly and completely helpless to battle the desire that he felt for her.

So he kissed her. Kissed her hard, held her face and angled her head just so he could take it deep. His tongue sliding against hers, stoking the fire in his midsection that left him shaken to his core.

And he didn't do shaken. He didn't do anything like this. "Kiss me back," he demanded.

And she whimpered, wrapping her arms around his neck. He felt the bag of burgers hit him square between the shoulder blades, but he didn't really care.

He arched his pelvis against hers, let her feel the intensity of his arousal.

"Chance…"

"Tell me," he said.

"Chance…"

"Tell me what you did," he said, reaching down and cupping her breasts, squeezing one, rubbing his thumb over her nipple until she gasped with desire.

"Tell me what you did, Juniper."

"I didn't… I didn't do anything."

He arched his hips forward, grinding the evidence of his arousal against the cleft between her thighs, and she shook, shuddered.

"You're a little liar," he said.

"And you," she said against his mouth, "are a fucking asshole."

"Am I? Am I the one who lied to a man that couldn't remember who he was?"

"Am I the person that is trying to steal somebody's land out from underneath them?"

"I told you to get a fucking surveyor, Juniper," he said, curling his fist into her hair and pulling, angling her head back as he kissed her deeper. "Did you think about doing that?"

"You pay for it," she spit, then launched herself up on her toes and kissed him again.

He picked her up, just a couple of inches off the ground, and walked them both backward into the house. He slammed the door behind them, grabbed the bag of hamburgers from her hands and flung them down onto the couch.

Then he set her back down, staring down into her eyes. "Too far," he said. "You went too far."

"I saved your ass, Chance."

"Well, thank you for not leaving me out there to get eaten by coyotes, what a fantastic example of your humanitarianism. You truly are the best of us, Juniper."

"Screw you," she said.

"I'd rather screw *you*," he said.

And he grabbed the top button on that EMT uniform and flipped it open.

Then he did the next button, and the next, revealing golden-brown curves that made his mouth water.

"You always knew it would end here, didn't you?" he asked.

"You're such a bastard," she said, reaching out, her hands working the buckle on his belt. She undid the snap on his jeans, then reached inside, and the breath hissed through his teeth that she curled her fingers around his cock, squeezing him tight.

"Such a bastard," she said, but this time the words had no heat.

And her mouth dropped open, a small whimper escaping. She licked her lips, then looked up at him. "You're so big," she said.

And that did it. That absolutely undid him. Juniper looking at him and talking about his size, the venom gone from her voice… There were spare few novelties left in the world for him.

He had experienced loss, grief, he'd had well

more than his share of sex, but this… This was a truly new experience.

And he hated that he was betraying to her that he was so damned basic. That all it took to get his engine revved was for a woman to say something like that.

Not a *woman*. *Her.*

It's the fact that it's her.

"And you are the sexiest little demon I've ever seen," he said. "Shame about your personality."

"Shame about yours," she said, still gripping him tight and running her hand up and down his aching shaft.

"Let's get you out of this," he said, undoing the rest of the buttons on her top and flinging it down to the ground.

Her bra was simple, black, but displayed her glorious cleavage to perfection.

He lowered his head, licking the plump skin there, tugging down one side of her bra and revealing her nipple, sucking it deep into his mouth until her head fell back and she gasped.

She held on to his head as he sucked, teased her. With his other hand, he smoothed down her back, moving to grab her ass, squeezing her as he continued to tease her.

He could feel her begin to tremble. Her whole body on a razor's edge.

"You're gonna call my name so many times that neither of us will ever forget it," he said against her mouth.

"I'll make sure to spell mine," she said. "That way it gets in there good."

He did away with the matching navy pants she was wearing, and with the bulky uniform dispensed with, he could see that she was all woman, all curves.

Her underwear did not match her bra, and there was something about that that got him hot.

This wasn't a woman who had been expecting to have sex.

Black bra, white panties with little red roses.

"Cute," he said. "I didn't take you for a delicate little flowers kind of girl."

"It's not that deep. I bought a package, white, beige and floral."

"You are something else," he said.

"Don't fall in love with me."

He laughed. And kissed her again. "No worries," he said. "I'm not in any danger. We're going to have a lot of fun, though."

And he hauled her up off the ground again, this time lifting her completely so that she could wrap her legs around his waist.

While he walked her back to her bedroom, she grabbed the back of his shirt and tugged it up over his head. He let go of her with one arm, then the other, so that she could free the entire garment. Then she cast it onto the ground. She put her hands on the center of his chest, running her fingers down his body.

"It is such a nice chest," she said.

"I like yours too." He reached around and unhooked her bra, freeing her breasts and revealing them to his gaze. "Fuck," he said. "You're so damn sexy."

"Good," she said, and she had that same wicked smile on her face that he felt on his own when she'd said he was so big.

There was just something about it. Knowing that the person who hated you more than anything was completely spellbound by your body. Couldn't do anything to fight this. Because, dammit, if they could, they would. She had done something that was unforgivable. But he didn't like her anyway.

Sure, for a minute, he thought he did. But then he remembered himself. And it had been different. It was all different.

And he wasn't worried about it.

He was going to have her.

He was going to have his way with her until neither of them could walk.

He flung her down onto the bed, then kicked off his boots and took the rest of his clothes off along with it.

Her eyes went round. She gripped the edges of her underwear, and she made them down her legs, leaving her spread out and naked for him on the bed.

He growled and came down over her. "Little witch."

"Asshole," she said, putting her hand on his face.

And then he kissed her. With all the pent-up hunger inside of him. And this wasn't as angry as the rest. Because he was past anger now. All the fire in his blood was desire. And he was desperate for wanting her. She sighed and arched against him, her legs falling open, and he put his hands between her thighs, stroking the wet seam of her body, moving his thumb in a circle over that sensitized bud there.

And then he pushed a finger into her, then another, working her as he kissed her. Until he couldn't take it anymore.

He didn't take a slow, leisurely trip down her body. He just moved quickly, dragging her hips up to his face and licking her deep, making her body arch up off the bed. "Yes," he said, lapping at her with all the need inside of him.

He tasted her, licked her, sucked her until she was sobbing, until she was begging. He pushed two fingers inside of her and stroked her until she whimpered. He added a third slowly and she started to shake, her thigh muscles trembling as he sucked her deep into his mouth while pushing deep.

And she broke. She grabbed hold of his hair, pulling hard as her internal muscles pulsed around his fingers. As her release ripped through her, seemingly going on and on.

He was so hard he could scarcely stand it.

He had never believed in blue balls before, but he did now.

If he didn't have her, he was going to combust. Or something was going to fall off. And he didn't want that.

"Please tell me you have some condoms," he said. "I don't have any of my shit."

"I do," she said.

She hurried off the bed and into the bathroom, and he heard her rummaging around. It took her a minute, but she finally returned with a strip of protection.

"It's been a while," she said. "I don't really need to just keep them by the bed."

"I'm not judging either way. I'm just glad that you have them."

It hadn't been a while for him. Or maybe it had. Maybe it had been forever. Maybe this was the first time. Maybe this was the only thing that mattered.

He wasn't sure anymore. Everything was mixed up and jumbled up inside of his head, and the only thing that really made sense was her.

She went back down onto the bed, and he took one of her arms and pinned it up over her head. Then he did the same with the second, the pose trapping her beneath him and raising her breasts up like an offering. He lowered his head to them again, sucked one briefly into his mouth, then another.

He positioned himself at the entrance of her body, and she was so tight and wet he groaned.

"Please," she begged. "Chance."

"Say it again."

"Please, Chance," she said.

And he thrust home. She arched up off the bed, a rough cry rising in her throat. And she met his every stroke, thrust for thrust.

Her nails digging into his skin as he drove them both to the edge of sanity.

Loyal Readers
FREE BOOKS Voucher

We're giving away THOUSANDS of FREE BOOKS

HARLEQUIN
DESIRE

THE TROUBLE
with Bad Boys

KATHERINE GARBERA
USA TODAY BESTSELLING AUTHOR

Sizzling Romance

HARLEQUIN
PRESENTS

Her Impossible
Baby Bombshell

USA TODAY BESTSELLING AUTHOR
DANI COLLINS

Passionate Romance

Don't Miss Out! Send for Your Free Books Today!

Get up to 4 FREE FABULOUS BOOKS You Love!

To thank you for being a loyal reader we'd like to send you up to 4 FREE BOOKS, absolutely free.

Just write "YES" on the Loyal Reader Voucher and we'll send you up to 4 Free Books and Free Mystery Gifts, altogether worth over $20, as a way of saying thank you for being a loyal reader.

Try **Harlequin® Desire** books featuring the worlds of the American elite with juicy plot twists, delicious sensuality and intriguing scandal.

Try **Harlequin Presents®** Larger-print books featuring the glamourous lives of royals and billionaires in a world of exotic locations, where passion knows no bounds.

Or **TRY BOTH!**

We are so glad you love the books as much as we do and can't wait to send you great new books.

So don't miss out, return your Loyal Reader Voucher Today!

Pam Powers

LOYAL READER
FREE BOOKS VOUCHER

▼ DETACH AND MAIL CARD TODAY! ▼

YES! I Love Reading, please send me up to 4 FREE BOOKS and Free Mystery Gifts from the series I select.

Just write in "YES" on the dotted line below then return this card today and we'll send your free books & gifts asap!

➡️ YES ⬅️

Which do you prefer?

| ☐ **Harlequin Desire®** 225/326 HDL GRGA | ☐ **Harlequin Presents® Larger Print** 176/376 HDL GRGA | ☐ **BOTH** 225/326 & 176/376 HDL GRGM |

FIRST NAME

LAST NAME

ADDRESS

APT.#

CITY

STATE/PROV.

ZIP/POSTAL CODE

EMAIL ☐ Please check this box if you would like to receive newsletters and promotional emails from Harlequin Enterprises ULC and its affiliates. You can unsubscribe anytime.

Your Privacy – Your information is being collected by Harlequin Enterprises ULC, operating as Harlequin Reader Service. For a complete summary of the information we collect, how we use this information and to whom it is disclosed, please visit our privacy notice located at https://corporate.harlequin.com/privacy-notice. From time to time we may also exchange your personal information with reputable third parties. If you wish to opt out of this sharing of your personal information, please visit www.readerservice.com/consumerschoice or call 1-800-873-8635. **Notice to California Residents** – Under California law, you have specific rights to control and access your data. For more information on these rights and how to exercise them, visit https://corporate.harlequin.com/california-privacy.

© 2021 HARLEQUIN ENTERPRISES ULC
™ and ® are trademarks owned by Harlequin Enterprises ULC. Printed in the U.S.A.

HD/HP-520-LR21

HARLEQUIN® Reader Service — **Here's how it works:**

Accepting your 2 free books and 2 free gifts (gifts valued at approximately $10.00 retail) places you under no obligation to buy anything. You may keep the books and gifts and return the shipping statement marked "cancel." If you do not cancel, approximately one month later we'll send you more books from the series you have chosen, and bill you at our low, subscribers-only discount price. Harlequin Presents® Larger-Print books consist of 6 books each month and cost $5.80 each in the U.S. or $5.99 each in Canada, a savings of at least 11% off the cover price. Harlequin Desire® books consist of 6 books each month and cost just $4.55 each in the U.S. or $5.24 each in Canada, a savings of at least 13% off the cover price. It's quite a bargain! Shipping and handling is just 50¢ per book in the U.S. and $1.25 per book in Canada*. You may return any shipment at our expense and cancel at any time — or you may continue to receive monthly shipments at our low, subscribers-only discount price plus shipping and handling. *Terms and prices subject to change without notice. Prices do not include sales taxes which will be charged (if applicable) based on your state or country of residence. Canadian residents will be charged applicable taxes. Offer not valid in Quebec. Books received may not be as shown. All orders subject to approval. Credit or debit balances in a customer's account(s) may be offset by any other outstanding balance owed by or to the customer. Please allow 3-4 weeks for delivery. Offer available while quantities last. **Your Privacy** – Your information is being collected by Harlequin Enterprises ULC, operating as Harlequin Reader Service. For a complete summary of the information we collect, how we use this information and to whom it is disclosed, please visit our privacy notice located at https://corporate.harlequin.com/privacy-notice. From time to time we may also exchange your personal information with reputable third parties. If you wish to opt out of this sharing of your personal information, please visit www.readerservice.com/consumerschoice or call 1-800-873-8635. **Notice to California Residents** – Under California law, you have specific rights to control and access your data. For more information on these rights and how to exercise them, visit https://corporate.harlequin.com/california-privacy.

▲ If offer card is missing write to: Harlequin Reader Service, P.O. Box 1341, Buffalo, NY 14240-8531 or visit www.ReaderService.com ▲

BUSINESS REPLY MAIL
FIRST-CLASS MAIL   PERMIT NO. 717   BUFFALO, NY

POSTAGE WILL BE PAID BY ADDRESSEE

HARLEQUIN READER SERVICE
PO BOX 1341
BUFFALO NY 14240-8571

NO POSTAGE
NECESSARY
IF MAILED
IN THE
UNITED STATES

And then when he couldn't hold on anymore, he pressed his face into her neck and bit her.

And that was when he felt her lose her grip.

Her climax took him off guard, the force of it tearing through him like a wildfire. Her internal muscles clenched tight around his cock, and he lost it completely.

He moved his hand down to her hips, gripped her tightly as he thrust into her three more times, hard and fast, before spilling himself.

"Juniper," he said, unable to hold back the exultation of her name. Unable to do anything but simply… Praise her.

He lay down beside her, his chest pitching with the effort of breathing.

"Hell," he said.

"I can't move," she said. "You killed me."

And then she laughed.

"What?"

"My sister said you would kill me."

"Your fucking sister knows?"

"My fucking sister *saw you*," she said. "I ended up having to tell her."

"You owe me," he said.

"I'm… I what?"

"I'm not kidding. You crossed the line."

"We have to talk about this right now. Have you ever heard of an afterglow?"

"I don't think you get an afterglow with hate sex," he said.

"Was it hate sex? Or was it just undeniable sex?"

"A good question," he said. Because he had to wonder if maybe it was more undeniable than he would like. He had to wonder if maybe they'd been headed this direction the whole time. So maybe not as directly, all things considered.

"In what way do I owe you?"

"You're going to have to come work for me."

"I am not working for Carsons," she said.

"You have no choice. You slept with me. You lied to me. And there are quite a few things I could do with that."

"Are you… Blackmailing me?"

He hadn't really intended to. And he didn't quite know what all was going on inside of him just at the moment.

But it seemed reasonable. It seemed reasonable, the idea that he would bring her to Carson land and force her to do the same amount of labor that he'd done for her.

Or maybe it's not that at all. Maybe you're just trying to get your own back because you spilled your guts about Sophie and now she knows.

"I'm not working for you."

"I could probably call the police, Juniper."

"And tell them what? You had amnesia and I made you work for me? Yeah. I'm sure that Deputy Morton would be very interested in that. She is my friend, by the way."

"Then maybe your grandfather would be interested to know that you have a hard time keeping your hands off me."

"You… You're horrible," she said. "I cannot believe that I just did that with you."

"You can't?"

Their eyes met, and she looked away.

"Maybe you should just do it because you feel bad."

"I will never feel bad for you. I will never feel bad for any Carson."

"Let me know when you have a day off coming up," he said.

She rolled out of bed and stepped away from him, and he watched the gentle jiggle and that rounded curve of her ass as she stalked into the bathroom.

She was soft. Curvy. He liked it.

And he hadn't had sex with her to enact any kind of revenge. It was just that it was… Convenient.

She came back in a moment later, fully dressed. "How about this?" she said. "I'll come work for you. I will debase myself as your farm girl. But in the end, you agree to look into what happened between our great-great-grandfathers. And into the way the card game happened. If your family has a record…"

"I'm sorry, I don't think you're in a position to negotiate," he said.

"Maybe not," she said.

And he realized that they were at the end of everything. Of common sense, of dignity. He had been filled with an insane amount of rage, and rightly so. But it had led here. And now he was trying to use it against her. And maybe they did need to settle it, once and for all. But his pride wouldn't allow him to do it for nothing.

"All right, Juniper Sohappy, you have yourself a deal."

"You know I don't have time to come work for you."

"I know. Maybe use some vacation time."

"You…"

"You'll get your evidence, if it exists."

"Good," she said.

"Get time off."

"Get out of my house," she said.

"Now… I'm going to need a ride," he said.

She reached over to the nightstand, grabbed her keys and threw them at him. "I'll have my sister drive me, and I'll pick up the truck tomorrow when I report for work."

"Well, then. See you bright and early."

And he began to collect his clothes, and he had a feeling it was going to take a hell of a long time to sort through everything that had happened over the last few days.

Seven

She had to submit for time off and she was furious about it. But that was a good thing, because when she wasn't furious she felt overcome by the memories of what it had been like to be in bed with Chance.

The way that he had touched her, the way that he had... The way that he had filled her.

And that bastard had gone ahead and proved her own fantasies were wrong. Oh, it had been intense. It had been angry. But he carried her right to bed, and there was something in that, when her previous, shame-filled fantasies had always been centered around them not making it to a bed.

No, it infuriated her.

And also left her hot and bothered in a way that...

Sex had never been like that for her.

Forget multiorgasmic, she had never even been consistently orgasmic. And even then, often it had felt muted.

She had always been more concerned about how she looked, the way that she was reacting. All these little things that really shouldn't matter, but did.

And she found herself stalking over to Shelby's house, because she was going to have to explain her absence. And she… Well, she would rather have Shelby be the keeper of the information, and not her parents. And definitely not her grandparents.

"Still alive, I see," Shelby said.

She laughed bitterly. "Oh yes. But he knows."

"Oh no," Shelby said. "What happened?"

And she felt… She didn't want to talk about sleeping with him.

Because what did it say about her? She had been… She had been angry and so turned on when they had been fighting. She should've resisted him, but it had never even entered her mind to do that. She had just… She had just wanted him. And what kind of insanity was that? Just wanting a man who so clearly hated her. The malice in his eyes as he had advanced on her…

But then he'd kissed her. And gradually the quality of the heat between them had changed.

Gradually it had become about something else.

And by the time he had buried his head between her legs and…

Well, she could honestly say no man had ever done that quite like that before.

He was a beast.

And she had… She had loved it. She had always sort of considered herself practical about sex. Not that she would say she wasn't sexual. She got the urge like anyone else. Just that it wasn't a driving factor in her life, or anything she needed all that frequently.

But after all that with him, she was ruminating on it quite a bit more than she would like to admit.

"Well, I am being blackmailed," she said.

Shelby sputtered over her coffee. "You're being blackmailed."

"I guess that's a little bit dramatic. But he is making me work for him. Tit for tat."

"Well," Shelby said. "All things considered… It could be worse."

"Don't tell me you're taking his side."

"There's not really a side here. You play games with dangerous predators and you win… Well, you win whatever the predator is going to do."

"You don't know anything about this. You don't know anything about predators."

She laughed. "Maybe not. But I'm smart enough to know I wouldn't screw around with one of the Carsons."

"Right. Well. So I'm just imagining the fact that your cheeks get pink when Kit Carson goes by?"

She felt guilty. She really did. Because Kit Carson was a closed subject, and Juniper knew it, and yet here she was, talking about him.

"There's nothing between me and Kit Carson," Shelby said.

"Doesn't mean you don't look at him."

"I'm not dead," Shelby said. "That's the thing."

And she knew that she was dancing dangerously close to things that she ought not to touch.

"Fine. I just wanted to let you know, in case anyone asked. I am doing some work on a friend's ranch."

"A friend."

"Well." She sighed. "And I'll get Chuck's clothes back for you."

"Thanks," Shelby said. "I probably shouldn't hold on to them."

"You love him," Juniper said.

"I do," Shelby agreed. "I do love him, but I think that that isn't… Isn't helping. It doesn't do anything. It doesn't bring him back." She shook her head. "Any more than hanging on to his clothes or his pocket knives or… Or anything."

"It doesn't make it go away," Juniper said.

"No," Shelby said. "It doesn't. It would give me more space, though."

"Well, I guess at a certain point you'll decide what you need more. His things or space."

"True," Shelby said. "Right now… I don't really need the space. You be careful."

"What do you mean? You keep acting like Chance

is dangerous. We may not like each other, we may be involved in a feud, but…"

"No, the problem is I think you do like him. I think you always have. You have a conflict with him. But if you didn't…"

"It doesn't matter. I do. Grandpa hated Chance's grandfather. Until Chance makes it right, what Grandpa feels like…"

"Why is it up to Chance to make it right? And why is it up to you to fix it? Your great-great-grandfather caused all this bullshit."

"It was Chance Carson's great-great-grandfather and…"

"Hey, maybe he cheated him. Maybe he took advantage. What happened happened."

"That's easy for you to say, Shelby. This isn't up to you."

"Why is it up to you?"

She nearly exploded. "Because I promised. I promised him. And I said it would be easy and I could do it. I have to be the one because there isn't another one."

Shelby looked like she pitied her then, and Juniper could hardly stand it. "If our great-great-grandfather couldn't fix it. Or our great-grandfather. Or our grandfather. Or our father… Why do you think you can?"

Because then she'd know. She was right.

She'd done right.

"Because," she said, knowing she sounded frustrated and childish. "Because somewhere, deep down, I kind of assume he *does* care about what's right."

"I see. And it's not just about the Carsons, it's

about him. That's what it always comes back to. The way the two of you fight about this."

"It does not always come back to the two of us."

"It does, Juniper. It always has. Like I said, what if there was no feud? How would you feel then?"

"It doesn't matter."

"You kissed him."

"Well, yes," she said, her cheeks going hot.

"And?"

"It doesn't matter. Because he is who he is, and I'm who I am. And all that matters is that this might finally settle things between us. He agreed to get the property assessed. Based on old records..."

"You don't have the money for that."

"He does. He agreed to pay."

Shelby arched a brow and crossed her arms. "I'm worried what that's gonna cost you."

"Again, you're acting like..."

"It's your emotions, Juniper. I am worried about your emotions. I am worried that you have feelings for this man. And if you spend more time with him, something is going to happen and..."

Juniper's face went hot.

Shelby's eyes narrowed. "Something already did. You're not telling me something."

"It doesn't matter."

And then her sister's eyes widened. Comically. "You *slept with him*."

"Maybe. Well, there was no sleep. He stormed out after."

"Oh."

And suddenly, Shelby took on the manner of an indecisive squirrel. Her body jerked one way, then another, and Juniper wondered what the hell was happening with her sister.

"What?"

"I'm trying to decide something."

"What are you trying to decide?"

"I'm trying to decide if I want to know the details."

"Why?"

"Because I would be lying if I said that I wasn't curious about…well. There are a lot of Carson men."

Juniper narrowed her eyes. "Kit. You are curious about Kit. And you think hearing about his brother will give you insight."

"Why are you fixated on Kit?"

"Because you're fixated on Kit. I'm not an idiot. He has made you into a little bit of a stuttering mess since you were sixteen."

Her sister's face flushed, but this time it was with anger. "I was with Chuck when I was sixteen. The fact that I got embarrassed around an inarguably cute boy is not an indicator of anything."

Except she thought it probably was. She thought it always had been.

But there was no having the discussion. And maybe there was really no point. Juniper had never been very good at letting things go. The entire incident with Chance being a prime example of that.

"Tell me you've never had a sex dream about him."

"Get out of my house," Shelby said, only a little bit kidding.

"It's really big," Juniper said.

Shelby bit her lip. "Thank God."

"Right?"

There would've been nothing sadder. Nothing sadder at all than evidence that all those tall, handsome men were over there and they were... Lacking.

But she could say with certainty, Chance was not lacking at all.

"It's just good to know," Shelby said pragmatically. "That there are some things in the universe that make sense."

"I guess. Though, if I hadn't made a very bad choice and slept with a Carson, I might've found it amusing if they had all been cursed with teeny-weenies."

"Yeah. But a handsome man is a handsome man. And a waste of all that...would be a waste of all that. Feud or not."

"Yeah. Fair," she said.

"I'll cover for you."

"Thank you."

"Don't have sex with him again."

"I won't. It was a onetime thing. The truth is, it had been... Brewing. And the whole explosion when he got his memory back was the tipping point. And I don't think it's going to combust like that again."

"It better not. Protect yourself."

"Aye, aye, captain."

And as she left her sister's house, she purposed in

her mind to let go of fantasies of Chance. She purposed in her mind to rid herself of impure thoughts entirely.

She was going to work. She was going to keep the goal in mind.

With any luck, this feud would finally be over. Or maybe it would still simmer beneath the surface, but she would be proved right.

And as far as she was concerned, Chance Carson could die mad.

Eight

"I don't see any cattle."

That was Chance's greeting when he got back to Evergreen Ranch.

"Well, that's because I didn't go get them," Chance said. "Where the hell is my horse, by the way?"

"Hell if I know," Kit said. "Keep track of your shit."

"Yeah, I don't know," Jace said.

"Is she here?"

"Why don't you know?" Boone asked.

Well, he was going to enjoy *this*.

"I don't know," he said, "because I have had amnesia."

His brothers exchanged a glance. Seated around the table outside one of the barns, where they all took their lunch, they had been eating sandwiches and planning the day when Chance showed up.

He had stopped off at his cabin and taken a very long shower.

Put on some of his own clothes that actually fit, and tried to make absolutely certain that he had his thoughts together.

"You do not have amnesia," Boone said. "That is idiotic. That's like the time we told Kit that Dad was going to sell him to a traveling band to play the washboard and set him out at the edge of the property at ten p.m. He believed it because he was eight. We're not eight."

"I did," he said. "I spent days not knowing who I was, and I don't know what happened to my horse."

His brothers looked at each other. "Seriously," Boone said.

"Seriously. I don't know what happened to my horse, who I can only assume ran back here. But I'm a little concerned about her."

"Well. I don't know. It's entirely possible one of the hands did something with her."

"Great," he said. "Not only did you assholes never try to contact me, and get concerned about me, you don't know where my horse is."

Flint frowned. "Where *have* you been?"

"It's a long story," he said. "However, it ends with the fact that Juniper Sohappy is going to be working here. She owes me."

"Well, I need to hear the long story," Kit said, kicking back in his chair. "Because you're claiming to have been struck down with amnesia and now I hear Juniper Sohappy is involved. So it is story fuckin' time."

This was the part he was looking forward to less.

"Fine. She found me, she rescued me. But I didn't remember who I was. And she told me that I was her ranch hand."

Boone just about fell out of his chair. Kit was laughing so hard that Chance thought he might choke, while Jace was shaking his head, his eyes wide. "Well, damn," Jace said.

"Yeah. So."

He noticed they were happy to believe the amnesia thing now.

"I knew she hated you," Boone said, wiping tears off his face, "but that is really something. So she held you hostage all this time?"

"Yeah. Torture every hour."

"Really." Boone and Flint looked at each other.

"Shut the fuck up," Chance said. But he couldn't even really be mad, because they were right.

He had in fact slept with her. That was in fact a thing that had happened.

"We'll behave ourselves," Flint said. "When she gets here. Unless you don't want us to. Which would be fair."

"She and I have an agreement."

He wasn't going to get into the whole thing with the card game and looking for evidence that may not exist.

Because then they really would ask what the hell he was doing.

Because why he had agreed to meet any of her demands, he really couldn't explain. She didn't deserve it. That was the thing. That was the bottom line. She didn't have any kind of high ground. She didn't have any kind of upper hand. It made no earthly sense that he was giving it to her.

"I'll see you guys around. I'll be devising torture for Juniper."

"Return torture," Boone said. "My favorite."

"You're a dick," Chance said as he walked away.

And right when he got to the main through road for the barn, Juniper pulled in.

"Howdy," he said when she rolled her window down. "Welcome to Evergreen Ranch."

"Thanks," she responded.

"You can park over this way."

Thankfully his brothers had cleared out by the time he got to the barn. He didn't want to deal with them on top of having to deal with her.

"All the trainees start here," he said.

She rolled her eyes, then rolled the window of the truck up. She killed the engine and got out, and his gut went tight at the sight of her.

She was wearing a tight black tank top and a pair of formfitting jeans.

Much more flattering than the EMT uniform.

And he knew what her body looked like underneath all that now.

Knew that the promise of the spark that had burned

between them all this time was barely even a preview of what it could be like between them.

He was a lot taller than her, nearly a whole foot, he reckoned. And yet they had fit together perfectly.

And he was trying to keep his mind on the task at hand, and not on her, but it was difficult. Because last night was still fresh in his mind.

"I'm investigating to see if my horse actually made it back," he said.

"Oh," she said. "I didn't know you fell off your horse."

"I did. I can't remember quite what happened. Something. Something must've spooked her. She's a good mount, and normally steady, but…"

They went into the barn and went down the stalls. Most of them were empty, because his brothers had taken their horses out for the day, but there she was.

"Geneva, you turncoat," he said. "You left me to die."

"Now, you leave her alone," Juniper said. "I think she's a discerning woman."

"She's not discerning of shit," Chance said, shaking his head. "She's a termite is what she is."

"I won't hear a word said against her."

"You can choose any of the horses that are left," he said. "Lefty is pretty good. Cheech has a bad temper."

"Well, so do I. I guess I'll settle for Cheech."

She did so, and while they were getting ready, she ran her hands over the horse lovingly. "Ex-rodeo horses?"

"For the most part. Not all."

"I never did know how I felt about the rodeo."

"Believe me when I tell you, nobody cares more about their animals than the people who breed them for those events. They're worth more than the cowboys. Trust me."

"I guess I can understand that. In the sense that I know a lot of people don't get that cattle ranchers care about cows more than just about anybody."

"Damn straight," he said. "We're connected to the way everything in the world works. To the way it's fueled. Life, death and the cost of all of it."

"I never would've thought we have something in common."

"Well, there you go, we have a couple things in common. Caring about our animals, and a mutual enjoyment of having sex with each other."

She frowned deeply. "How do you know I enjoyed it?"

"Please. You were basically putty."

"Maybe I'm easy," she said.

"Somehow, I don't think so. Somehow, I think you're a little bit of a tough nut, Juniper Sohappy. And I think I cracked you."

"Please. Men really do think highly of themselves."

"I think pretty highly of you too."

"So highly that you're forcing me to do manual labor for you?"

"Payback for the work I did for you."

"Fine," she said. "That's fair enough."

"Yeah. Sometimes I am. And if you would stop being mad at me for the sake of it, you might see that."

He got on his horse, and she mounted behind him, and the two of them took off, with him leading the way.

They walked the horses down over a bare rocky ridge that ran along the river.

This was high desert.

The rocks ran the gamut from pale tan to adobe red.

The sagebrush that was scattered throughout the landscape was scrubby and vile. The deer liked to eat it, but it gave them a particular flavor that Chance had never been fond of.

Because of course he actually did know the taste of venison, the taste of elk and the different regions where they tasted different, because of what they ate.

Because now he understood himself, and his memories, and it was no longer a mystery.

He felt a strange… A strange stab of envy for the man he had just been two days ago who hadn't known a damn thing. Who had been strangely excited by the things that he knew, and unencumbered by… Everything. The only thing he had known for sure was Juniper.

And that had been interesting.

To say the least.

Great. He missed being a simpleton. That was really something.

He shook his head.

"There's a whole bunch of lava rock down in here, and you can find agates," he said. "Me and my brothers used to spend hours down here hunting rocks. It was our favorite spot to go."

"I can imagine you running wild around here. And getting into all kinds of scrapes," she said.

"Oh hell, yeah. One time Boone got bitten by a rattlesnake."

"Really?"

"Yeah. Oh man, he held off on telling Mom and Dad as long as possible, because he was sure that he was going to get his hide tanned. And he was right. Dad was so pissed off."

"He was mad that Boone got bitten by a rattlesnake. At *Boone*."

"Yeah. We weren't watching. We weren't being responsible. We knew better."

"Still, that seems a little odd."

"It's just that they had so much to worry about, what with…"

He cut himself off. Because he didn't really intend to talk about Sophie.

He never did. It was just that he had already told her, in a roundabout way. And that was the problem.

He had already explained certain aspects of that part of his past, even without the details.

And it had made him feel freer now.

"Well, at the time my parents had a lot on their plate."

"Right. Well, I never got bitten by a snake. But

Shelby and I used to run all over the ranch too. It's funny, how we didn't really run into each other."

"You stay to your side, we stay to ours. It stands to reason."

"Yeah." She chewed her bottom lip. "My grandfather really hated yours."

"A lot of people did," Chance said. "He was a difficult bastard. It doesn't surprise me that your grandfather hated him. I'm not sure that any of us were ever especially fond."

"Really?"

He shook his head. "Yeah. I don't know. To hear my dad tell it, he was mean. Mean as a snake."

"That isn't how I imagined you would feel. And if that's true…why do you care so much about the land? I know why I do. I love my grandfather, what matters to him matters to me."

"Because we're not carrying this on for him," Chance said. "We're carrying it on for us. To be more, bigger, better than the name he established for us. To be stewards of the land and everything that inhabits it." He grinned. "To get rich."

"Ha!" She belted that laugh and it echoed around them.

"Hey, in my estimation, my grandfather did one valuable thing. He had my father. And whatever his father was like, I don't know, but it's because of them that we are here. My mom and dad… They're good parents. Getting mad about rattlesnakes notwithstanding. They love us."

"Yeah. So do mine. We just want different things. We care about different things."

"You care about the ranch," he said.

"Yes," she said. "Just about to the exclusion of everything else, if I'm honest."

"Why do you care about it so much?"

"I remember once in school I was doing a group project, and this kid got mad at me for having an opinion. And he told me to go back to where I belong. You know, my country." She held her arm out in front of her, showing her brown skin. "And I didn't know what to say at the time. All these things stuck in my throat, chief of which were how stupid he was. But... I realize that the ranch was where I was from. It rooted me. Grounded me. And even when people were ignorant or assholes or whatever... They can't take that from me. I belong here. I love it here."

Chance's stomach turned. "You might've told him to go back to where he came from."

She laughed. "Yeah. I thought about it later. Unfortunately, at the time I was just... Shocked. And sad. But the truth is, even though I didn't give him the thousand comebacks that I have inside of me now, I found my sense of resolve that day."

"I'm sorry that happened to you."

"Don't you think there's a little bit of that in this whole dispute?"

He stopped his horse and turned to face her. "Not for me."

"With our grandparents."

He looked surprised. "I don't… Probably. Probably. I can't say no."

"I think your grandfather, your great-grandfather, thought they deserved it more. Because they think they're more important."

"I'm sorry," he said. "It never occurred to me."

"Why would it?"

The simple question was a stinging indictment.

"Look, this is dumb. Why don't we figure out how to share?"

"No," she said. "I want to know. I really want to know. If you have paperwork that says anything about the ownership transfer, I want to see it. If you have family history. I don't want you to give me something because you feel guilty. And if…if he lost it fairly, if there's a way to know that…" She sucked in a breath. "I'll buy it back."

"You don't have the money," he said pointedly, and he saw her flinch as he did.

"I know. But I'll figure it out."

"What if there are no answers, anywhere?"

"There have to be some," she said. "Talking helps."

"Usually we just end up yelling."

"Yeah, I guess this is a step toward being functional adults. What a novel concept."

"We behaved like adults the other night," he pointed out.

And he regretted that, because he didn't need to bring it up. It just made it far too easy to imagine everything that had passed between them. And how damned good it was.

"Right," she said. "Except the aftermath."

"You have to admit," he said, because the reminder of her behavior brought him right back to reality, if nothing else would, "that what you did was…"

"All right. Lying to you wasn't my best move. But honestly, I couldn't tell you everything. You're not supposed to do that, because of shock. I needed you to have realizations on your own. Also, I sat up with you all night, I made sure that you were okay. I didn't leave you out in the middle of that field."

"I know," he said.

"What bothers you the most? That you did some labor for free? Or that I had to take care of you? Because I think maybe that's part of the problem. That and the fact that maybe you don't hate me."

"If I don't hate you, then you really don't hate me," he said.

"Well, I had to see you as a human being for a few days."

"Must've been a trial," he said.

"No. It wasn't. That's the problem."

"Well, I didn't know who you were."

"I wanted you to understand," she said. "I wanted you to understand why it was important. Not with all of what you think you know sitting there in your head. So I'm sorry if I made a weird choice. I'm sorry if I made a bad choice. But the land means the world to me. My grandfather means the world to me."

"And what would your grandfather say if he knew about us?"

"There's not an us," she said.

"I meant the fucking, Juniper, but I was trying to be a gentleman."

"He'd die," Juniper said, looking at him straight on. "Then and there. My grandfather will not be knowing about us. Not ever. He can't. I've given up too much to have a romp in the sack ruin my relationship with him."

"A romp in the sack? Wow."

"Oh, don't give me that, it's not like sex is sacred to you."

He looked at her long and hard, and what he hated most was that the word she'd used just now felt more right for this thing between them than any other he could think of.

He said nothing. He just snorted. "Well, I'm not in any hurry to spread it around."

"My sister knows," Juniper said. "But I can't keep anything from her. It doesn't work."

"My brothers know too, but it's not because they're insightful, it's just because they're assholes, and I didn't tell them anything. But they're going to think what they think no matter what. And they've always thought that…"

"They've always thought what?"

Sacred.

No, just sex. And sex he'd wanted for a long time,

in fact. Maybe that was why it was notable. Maybe that was the only real reason why.

"They've always thought that I wanted you."

"I see," she said. "And are they right?"

"What do you think?"

"What's your favorite spot on the whole ranch?" she asked.

He looked around and pointed down at the watering hole below. "That spot. All the good agates are there. And you can jump right in from those rocks. And the water goes way over your head. You feel like you're never going to touch the bottom. We used to play here all the time."

"It's nice," she said.

"Yeah. That's one of the last memories I have of all of us together. Before Buck…"

"What happened to Buck? I barely remember him, because he's older."

"He had that accident. He… He didn't want to stay after that."

He could never understand his brother's decision to leave.

Buck hadn't been the one drinking. He'd been badly injured all the same.

But it had something to do with his friend's death, he knew that.

But he had never understood what required Buck to leave home, to leave his entire family when they all would've supported him. But it was like he just didn't want to be here anymore.

And his absence had created some strange, hard feelings around town.

Especially with the family of his friend.

"Yeah. It's been rough without him. But I have a surplus of brothers."

"Well, you were all close."

And he thought about Sophie again, in spite of his best efforts.

"Yeah," he said. "We are close. We don't take family for granted. You can't take family for granted when…"

He stopped talking. And she didn't push him.

"How close are we to the border of your land?"

He knew she would know.

"Not far. Maybe two hundred yards."

"I want you to show me your favorite spot."

"I haven't done any work so far," she pointed out.

And he realized that he'd lost the thread of what today was supposed to be. He was supposed to be punishing her or something. He was supposed to be making her work. And they should've gone the rest of the way along this trail to get to the fence that needed fixing. But they could also do it later. They could do it later and it would be just fine.

But suddenly none of it seemed as important as this.

And it wasn't just because he was attracted to her, though he was. There was something else.

Something about the way the sun glinted off of her hair, and the way she smiled. Or the way she frowned.

There was just something about her.

"Show me," he said.

"Okay," she responded. "If you really want me to."

"I do."

She moved her horse forward, leading the way, jogging the animal down the side of the trail.

He laughed and took off after her. It was an easy ride. Not for beginners. It was for people like them, who knew what they were doing, knew the land and knew how to push the limits.

"You actually ride in the rodeo?" she asked when they were on a flatter part of the trail, moving into the more lush part of the land, pine trees suddenly becoming thicker and more prevalent.

"Yep," he said. "I can't say that I was the best. But I had a good time. Saddle bronc, mostly. That is generally my family's game."

"Oh. Not bulls."

"Boone rode bulls."

"Maybe I should've slept with Boone."

He shot her a look, and she grinned.

"Oh, so it's like that," he said.

"I'm a woman of discerning tastes," she said.

And he didn't think they had ever gone this long without acting like they were going to kill each other. So that was something.

They pushed their way through the trees, and the trail narrowed. "This is out way far away from anywhere my parents ever go to. And my grandpa quit moving through the whole property a long time ago. His mobility just isn't what it used to be. But this was my and Shelby's secret spot. The trees seem to grow over the trail, like a rounded entrance into some kind of enchanted world, and we imagined that if you were a child, that was exactly what you would see."

Especially what two girls would see.

"We always said there were fairies," she said. "There was a movie about that. Fairies in an English garden? And we were obsessed with it. And we used to imagine that they were here. I love this place."

There were purple flowers and ferns growing beneath the trees, and it was just entirely different to the landscape they had just come from.

There was running water nearby, and it took him a while to realize that it was a stream. It probably fed into the larger river that they had just come from.

And at the end of the stream was a little pool. "Not deep enough to jump in," she said. "But perfect for floating. Which is what we used to do."

"It's beautiful," he said.

"This place means so much to me," she said.

Then she got a mischievous glint in her eye, turned around and pulled her shirt up over her head.

She didn't know what she was thinking. Stripping while still on the back of a horse. It was crazy. And she had decided that she wasn't going to touch him again. Because it was foolishness. Absolute lunacy.

Because it wasn't anything that she needed to

do, and it was in fact something she absolutely shouldn't do.

But then, she didn't know why they were out spending time together. Riding around their favorite childhood spots rather than working or sniping.

And then she'd done that.

Oh well. She was committed now. She dismounted, unhooked her bra and threw it down where the shirt was. Then she stripped off the rest of the way and slipped into the translucent green water. It was like an emerald here under the trees, and the still pool with its large rounded stones at the bottom had always ignited her imagination. Had always made her feel like she was part of something wonderful. Part of something bigger than herself.

Part of something magic.

Her grandmother believed so strongly that there were things in the world that no one could understand. That nature itself had breath, and it was constantly speaking to them, flowing through them.

And it was here that Juniper could feel that for herself. Here that she felt touched in a spiritual way. And she had brought Chance to this spot. She really didn't know what she'd been thinking.

She felt vulnerable, exposed, and it wasn't just because she was naked.

"Join me?" she asked.

He got off his horse and pulled his shirt up over his head, revealing that delicious body to her gaze.

How could she ever go back? To hating him. She wanted to. It was simple.

Even just admiring his body, she had hated him.

But now he had touched her. And he was a generous lover, she couldn't overlook that. And what it said about him.

He wasn't a man who just took. He was a man who gave with talented fingers and a wicked tongue. He was a man who seemed to derive as much pleasure from hers as he did from his own.

That's just sex. It has nothing to do with the content of his character.

Well, that was a good reminder. But it wasn't doing much to penetrate her thinking right now.

He was completely naked in a moment, and then he joined her in the pool, his eyes intent on hers.

"Normally, I wouldn't be too thrilled about being in a pool of cold water in front of a beautiful woman. But thankfully, your beauty far outweighs the cold."

"Well. That is… Bizarrely flattering," she said.

"In the absence of anything else, always take bizarrely flattering."

"I'm not sure what to make of this," she said. "Given that you're my mortal enemy and all."

"Yeah, why me specifically?"

She knew the answer to that question. Because she was supposed to hate the Carsons, and from the first moment she had ever seen Chance Carson, hate was not the dominant emotion. She had been fascinated by him. She had been completely and utterly transfixed from day one, and there was something about the directive given to her by her grandfather, and that feeling that had made her feel violently angry with him in that first moment. When she had been eight and he was ten.

She remembered it so clearly. It may not make sense. And it may not be fair, but it was the truth.

She had liked him, and she wasn't allowed to. And she loved her grandfather more than she loved any other person on earth, and wanting a Carson was a violation of their family. Of their name.

Of all the promises she'd made to be worthy of being the one who took over the family legacy.

So she had done her best to turn that all into anger. She had done her best to turn it all into outrage.

But it hadn't worked. At least, not consistently.

And here she was. Naked in the water with him again.

"Chance…"

"You're beautiful," he said, closing the distance between them. And he kissed her lips, the heat of his body cutting through the icy water and making her tremble.

He wrapped his strong arms around her, crushing her breasts to his chest. "Dangerous," he gritted against her mouth.

"Why?"

"I don't have a condom."

"I'm on the pill," she said. "As long as you're… As long as you're good."

He nodded. "Yeah."

"Me too."

The fact of the matter was, she always doubled up

on her protection. This felt alarming and like a step into something new. But she wanted him. And she didn't want to wait for him. Because if they waited, they might come to their senses. If they waited, then they might realize that they shouldn't do this.

But she didn't want that realization. She wanted to feel him against her. Inside of her. She wanted to kiss him until neither of them could breathe. She wanted to chase down her pleasure with him.

Only him.

"I always use…"

"Me too," she said.

He understood. He didn't say anything, but he understood. That she'd never let a man do this before. And she felt breathless with the anticipation of it.

She waited for him to shift their positions and surge inside of her, but he didn't. Instead, he angled his head and kissed her. It was maddeningly, achingly slow, something completely different to the way they had come together in anger only recently. It was painful, almost. The care that he took with each corner of her lips. To make sure he kissed every inch. And then he began to look into her. Slowly. She moaned as he took the kiss deeper and deeper. As the desire between them became a burgeoning flame, and he kept it banked. It was the control. The absolute, maddening control that got her.

Because she felt like she was going to vibrate out of her skin, and he seemed to enjoy it. Didn't seem bothered. Not in the least.

His big hands roamed over her body, all of her curves, and he made them feel beautiful. Made them feel precious. She wasn't toned. Wasn't insanely physically fit, but she liked the way that it felt when he squeezed her tight; he made her softness feel sexy, and it was a novelty.

It was more than a novelty. She couldn't pretend that's all it was. Some simple fascination and nothing more. No. It was everything.

This moment was everything.

She moved her hands down his chest, his damp chest hair. He was just really beautiful.

And she was going to take this moment and drink it all in. Drink him in, because she didn't know if it would ever happen again. She didn't know if she would come to her senses. She should... Go now. She should come to her senses and put a stop to all of this. But she really didn't want to.

No. She wanted to savor it. To live in it.

And so she would. Now. Because now they were past the point of no return. Now there was no going back.

It didn't matter what anyone would think. Because it was only the two of them, here in the fairy grove, here in this place that was the closest she had ever gotten to showing any other person the deepest part of her heart.

She wondered if he realized. She wondered if he knew.

She watched as her fingertips skimmed over his

ab muscles, over the ridges and dips and hollows in those beautiful, corded muscles.

He was hard. Solid from all the work that he did. And she loved the contrast between their bodies.

Loved that he was masculine to her feminine. And she couldn't recall ever having luxuriated in that before.

She didn't think about her femininity much. It didn't matter to her.

He deepened the kiss, pulling her up against him, and she parted her thighs, wrapping them around his waist and moving her hips restlessly against him, trying to do something to soothe the ache there.

"Be patient," he said, nipping her lip.

"No," she said. "I'm not patient. I want you."

"Say my name."

And she realized that if there was ever a taboo fantasy, for her, this was it. It had been.

"I want you, Chance Carson."

It couldn't be any more blatant if she had asked him to take her on their disputed property.

He shifted their positions, and she felt the blunt head of his arousal pressing up against the entrance to her body. Then he surged inside of her, bare and hot, and she could tell even there in the water like this. She gasped. And his eyes met hers, intense and beautiful. And it terrified her then, how well she knew that face. How close it was to hers, and how much she wanted it to stay that way.

She wasn't really in conflict with herself, not any-more. And she had spent a whole lot of time wanting to see him only so they could fight, while the underlying issue was that she wanted to see him.

But she wasn't lying to herself. Not now. She just wanted to be close to him.

He began to move, his movements hard and intense, his mouth set into a firm line as he began to push them both closer and closer to paradise.

She gripped his shoulders, digging her fingernails into his skin, digging her heels into his thighs as she was pressed firmly against the rock wall of the pool while he took her.

She put her hands on his face and his jaw went slack, his thrusts getting harder, more intense. And all she could do was cling to him. This man. Her storm, her porch, and how could one person be both? It didn't make any sense. And she wished for a moment that she could be the one with amnesia. That she could just forget absolutely everything and have this moment. But he was Chance, and it was complicated. And there was never a scenario where it wouldn't be.

And it was just… It was too much. It was all too much.

And still, her climax rose inside of her. Threatening like an impending storm.

And she knew that if it broke open, it would drown her completely. But she didn't have the strength to deny him. Didn't have the strength to turn back now.

Then he kissed her and began to whisper against her mouth. Dirty promises that shocked her, that amped up her arousal. That made her slicker still and created a delicious friction between their bodies.

She met his every thrust, and when they went over the edge, it was together. And he spilled inside of her on a growl, the unbearable intimacy of the moment creating aftershocks within her.

And he didn't draw away from her when he was finished. Rather, he stayed like that, looking at her, stroking her hair back away from her face.

"I promise I really did mean to give you work to do today."

"Well, now I can't work," she mumbled, resting her forehead on his shoulder. "I don't think I can walk."

He chuckled. "It's touch and go for me too."

Then they both turned their heads at the same moment, looking at the horses, who were standing there placidly. "I can honestly say I haven't performed a live sex show for a pair of horses before," he said.

She laughed. "That kind of surprises me, given that you are a rodeo cowboy. I would've thought there was ample opportunity for you to be playing around with women in various paddocks."

"Hell, no," he said. "I'm a grown-ass adult past the age of having to have sex in strange places. I have a house, I have a bed, I have money for hotel rooms."

"That's awfully mature of you."

"Apparently, I'm not all that mature with you."

"Well, we've known that."

"I guess so." He sighed heavily. "What are we going to do about this?"

She lifted a shoulder. "Burn it out."

"Makes as much sense as anything."

And maybe on the other side of that, none of this would be there. Not the simmering anger or the burning desire. She could handle that. Lord knew she would actually be much happier.

She moved away from him, swimming to the shore and going to gather her clothes.

It was harder this time. Without the cloak of anger to do away with the tender feelings left behind by the connection created during sex.

Not that she'd ever been superaware of it before. It was worse, she decided—or better, she supposed, depending on how you wanted to look at it, but worse was the best descriptor for when it was with Chance—when it felt amazing. When you had an orgasm together. Because she felt somehow united with him in his pleasure, rather than an observer of his superior, easy-seeming male pleasure, which was how it had always been in the past. She was a participant. And he didn't go to where he couldn't bring her along.

A strange thing that it was with Chance she had found that.

"We ought to maybe go repair a fence or something," he said.

She laughed hollowly, tugging her shirt back over her head and then deciding to go hunt around for her shoes.

He was halfway dressed, and by the time she found her shoes, he had completed the job.

"Yeah. I guess that would be the responsible thing to do. If your version of revenge is just give me multiple orgasms, I have to say, it's not very good revenge."

"My bad," he said.

"Did you just say *my bad*? What year is it, and how old are you?"

He grinned. "Sorry."

She didn't know what to do with him when he was like this either. Good-humored and light and in general enjoyable rather than a big pain in her ass.

It was making compartmentalization nearly impossible. Because he wasn't just a little bit different when they were in the throes of passion.

He was a little bit different all around. Like they were finally able to drop some kind of guard they normally had up when they were with each other. And it made her wonder if he saw her as different too.

"I suppose we should go back and work on the fence now," he said.

"That would have been easier before you killed me," she said.

"Sorry," he responded, grinning. He did not look sorry.

She narrowed her eyes, but she couldn't really be mad. Mostly because the sex had been so good.

"I don't know very much about you," he said.

"You've known me forever."

"Yeah, I guess. But I don't really know much about you."

She realized the same was true of him.

"I don't know. I had a pretty normal childhood."

"Except people were gross to you at school sometimes."

"Yeah. But I don't really know any different than that. I'm tough, I was raised to be tough. We both were. I have both my parents, and I have my grandparents. We have it pretty good."

"But that's not the extent of it, is it? That's just surface stuff."

"It's all I really know about you."

"I want to know about the men in your life," he said.

She frowned. "There aren't any notable men in my life."

"Good," he said, his gaze assessing.

"What do you care?"

"I don't know. But I do."

"What about you? What about the women in your life?"

"I've never been serious about anyone. On purpose. I'm a ho."

"Well, points for honesty," she said, laughing.

"I never wanted anything permanent." He shook his head. "My parents do all right, especially with their lifestyle. Living out of an RV for part of the year while my dad travels around for the rodeo. But we've made it into our thing. Something we can rally around. I'm like you. I have both my parents… I guess in the end that makes me pretty lucky."

"Who was the little girl?" She shouldn't be asking this, because he had told her when he didn't remember anything, and it didn't really feel fair to fling this at him now.

"Yeah. So we came to that part. I'd rather we talk about how I'm probably the best sex you've ever had?"

She rolled her eyes. "Settle down, boy, you're all right."

"Why haven't you found anyone?"

"I told you already."

"That feels like an excuse."

"It's not an excuse. It's my life. What I want and what I dream of doing isn't an incidental. It's everything."

He nodded slowly. "My sister Sophie," he said. "We were close to the same age. She was always very sick. We loved her. I mean, we just doted on her. It was really something. The only girl among all those boys. We couldn't play with her, not the way that we could play with each other, because we had to be really careful with her. But it was all right. Nobody minded. Boone used to carry her around on his shoulders. Buck and Kit made a little cart just for her. With a princess canopy on it. She was in and out of the hospital all the time. And one time… She went and she never came back. And I remember… I remember standing in front of the hospital, in front of the doors, and my dad was grabbing my jacket sleeve and telling me to go inside, telling me to go visit. I couldn't. I couldn't go in. I just was frozen. Was some kind of terror that I couldn't quite sort out. But it was real, and it had me completely shaken. So I waited in the car, and then my sister died. She never came out of that hospital, and I wasn't brave enough to go in."

She hadn't expected that. She would've thought that anything that serious she would know about. She would've thought that it would've been something that people spoke of.

"Callie came along sometime after. And at first I was afraid. Afraid of what might happen to her. But she was this rowdy, rambunctious delight."

"But you can't replace somebody that you've lost. Not like a straight-out trade."

He shook his head. "No. It couldn't be clearer that they weren't the same person. It's funny, it's been so long. But I remember her on her birthday, and I remember how old she would've been. And you know Callie… She's great. My mother wanted that little girlie girl, though. And Callie isn't that. She ran roughshod with us over everything."

"I'm so sorry," Juniper said, feeling everything inside of her twist and turn onto its head.

She really didn't know him. She had never allowed him to be a full person. Not ever. She had always just seen him as her sworn enemy.

"It's all right. It's been a long time, like I said."

She thought of Shelby, and Chuck. "All time does is change wounds," she said. "Makes them into something different. It doesn't take them away, or turn you back into the person you were before. I know it isn't the same, but my brother-in-law was a lot like a brother to me. He and Shelby were together from the time I was fifteen. And he was always around. I can't remember my life without him. And then he was gone. She's devastated by it. She'll never be the person she was before. He was her other half. And then… I don't know. There's my grief. Which is real, but it isn't hers."

He hung his head. "Sharing grief can be a good thing," he said. "But there is something about it. When someone else feels it also much more than you. When someone else has a claim to the greater grief in the moment. But it doesn't make yours any smaller. It just means you're afraid of hurting them with yours."

"It must've been hard to watch your parents go through that."

"Yeah," he said. "It was. And my brothers. And it's been hard to watch Callie too in some ways. I envy her. Because she was never touched by the grief of it, not personally. But some of it… Did a decent enough job of messing her up. Because you know… You can't replace what you've lost."

She felt bruised for him. Cracked open inside.

"I'm sorry, I really didn't know."

He looked into the distance. Like he might find answers there, or at least find some break in the intensity between them. "It happened before we came here."

"Well, how inconvenient that you're a human being." She tried to say it with a laugh but she couldn't.

He aimed a lopsided grin at her. "I hate to be an inconvenience."

They got back on their horses and began to go back to the ranch. They found that fence line and set about to repairing it. "You're the best I've ever had," she said, because it felt a fair trade after he'd shared this.

"Tell me more," he said.

"I dunno. I thought sex was all right, but not worth jumping up and down over. I haven't always been able to…"

"You mean to tell me you were sleeping with guys who couldn't make you come?"

"Yeah, but I figured women don't really expect to come every time."

"Honey, I expect a woman with me to come every time. More than once."

"Well, so far, promise fulfilled. So, thank you for that."

"You're welcome."

She looked up and smiled at him, and her stomach went a little bit tight. And she didn't even feel like fighting it, or telling herself it shouldn't be like this. That it shouldn't be so easy to like him, or work his dadblasted Carson land.

She liked being beside him.

And she let it be.

When they finished the fence, it was dinnertime, and her hopes of sneaking away were dashed.

Because all of his brothers were sitting outside at a table in front of the barn, with a big dinner spread in front of them.

"What's this?"

"We had dinner sent up from the fancy hotel."

She blinked. She forgot sometimes that the Carsons were rich. Rich enough to cater a random dinner.

"Hey," one of them said. "Come join us."

She looked at Chance. He shrugged. "You're hungry?"

"Obviously."

And her stomach fluttered, because of course she was obviously hungry because they had burned so many calories not just fixing the fence, but with the activities from the swimming hole.

"Well, sit down and eat."

"Did you really order food from a fancy hotel just for a random dinner?"

"Yeah," Boone said. "I'm starving. And pot roast, mashed potatoes and dinner rolls sounded like the ticket to me."

"I guess with this many of you to feed…"

"Oh, my mom gave up being the person that tried that a long time ago. When we were high schoolers she resorted to basically throwing bologna our direction and running the other way."

"That's a lie," Kit said. "She threw bologna packages our direction and said make it your damn self."

Her stomach growled, and she took her seat at

the table, Chance seated alongside her, his thigh touching hers.

The brothers were loud and boisterous, and she hadn't actually spent time with them in a group since school. Even then, it had been more being adjacent to them than actually being in the middle of them.

They were a lot. A lot of personality, a lot of tall, handsome cowboy.

And she couldn't pretend anymore that she was immune.

She looked over at Kit. Kit, who she knew Shelby was attracted to. And she couldn't blame her. He was a handsome man, though he didn't do for her what Chance did. That was the thing. Objectively, every single one of the Carson men was stunningly attractive, with mixed and matched features from each other, hair ranging from dark brown to near blond. Brown eyes, hazel eyes, charming smiles, large hands.

But it was more than just finding him handsome. It was… Some kind of chemistry that seemed to defy everything else.

"I don't think I have ever seen you when you weren't scowling," Flint said.

"Well, normally I have something to scowl about if I'm around this many Carsons. But you're feeding me. So I'm not going to be a bitch."

Flint laughed and tossed another dinner roll her way. She caught it and started to slather it with butter.

And when she was done, she realized that she was smiling, and laughing, and eating seconds of berry pie while Jace encouraged her to put all the whipped cream that was left in the can over the top of it.

It was weird to recognize that they were a family. Like hers. That she had more in common with them than not. It had been so easy to make them enemies. To paint them something other, something less, than her own family. But here they were, sitting together, eating together, being immature at each other. It was just so shockingly normal. When they got up from the table, Chance put his hand on her lower back, and she stiffened. He dropped his hand, as if he had sensed the reaction.

They got closer to her truck, and he looked at her. "You want to spend the night?"

She laughed. She couldn't help it.

"What?"

"I haven't been asked for a sleepover in quite some time."

"Do you need to get your mom's permission?"

"They wouldn't give it."

"Then it's best if we don't ask."

"You are going to get me in a lot of trouble," she said.

"You started the trouble."

"Maybe we need to make sure your head injury didn't dramatically change your personality."

"No. Sleeping with you might have done that."

She flushed. "I have to go home and grab some things. I won't be a minute."

"I know. We're neighbors, after all."

Yes. They were neighbors. Feuding ones at that.

And she would do well to remember that. Because at the end of the day, no matter how much the Carsons were like the Sohappys, no matter how much she liked him, no matter how much fun it was to kiss him, no matter how exhilarating it was to have him inside of her, her grandfather would never get over the betrayal. And that was something that could simply never happen.

Nine

It had been two weeks of sneaking around with Juniper while she worked his land. And he really enjoyed it. He did.

But he'd been thinking. A lot. About the proposed endgame of all of this. He wasn't angry at her, not anymore. It was impossible to be. But what he wanted was to speak to her grandfather. He had decided that that was what he had to do.

What had become clear to him was that the biggest issue between him and Juniper was they could only see things one way. They saw the way their great-grandfathers had seen things, and had passed down that perception. And he was completely mired in that. He had to hear their side of the story. He needed to speak to her grandfather.

He could tell her, but…

He didn't want her to worry or have unnecessary anxiety about it, because he knew she was so protective of that relationship.

He'd be careful.

Because he was being careful with her.

He pulled up to the old farmhouse that was situated nearest the road on the ranch. There were two old cars in the driveway, and everything around the property was immaculate. No leaves, no debris. No nothing. The porch was spotless, with hanging plants all around.

Everything showed its age, but it also showed the incredible care that the owners put into it.

He parked, then walked up the steps, pausing for a moment before knocking firmly on the door.

He heard dogs barking, and then the shuffling of feet. The door opened to reveal a tiny gray-haired woman who was wearing a denim housedress and had her hair back in a low ponytail. "Yes?"

"Mrs. Sohappy," he said. "I was hoping I might be able to speak to Mr. Sohappy."

"Ron is sitting in his chair," she said. "What's your name?"

"I'm Chance Carson. I wanted to ask him a few questions."

The woman's eyes narrowed. "A Carson." Then the door slammed in his face, and he heard those same footsteps moving away from the door.

Well. Shit. Juniper hadn't been kidding. Her grandparents really did hate the Carsons, and he couldn't just show up and start talking to them, apparently.

He turned and started to walk down the steps, but then he heard the door open again. "Where you going?"

"I thought I wasn't welcome."

"I had to see if you were welcome," she said. "I wouldn't say *welcome*. But he will speak to you."

He nodded. "Thank you."

He walked back up the steps and followed the woman into the house. "I'm Anita," she said.

"It's nice to meet you, Anita," he said.

"We'll see if it's nice to meet you, Chance Carson."

He walked through a narrow hall and into a sitting room, where an old, gray-haired man was sitting in a mustard-yellow recliner. "What is it you want, Chance?" The man's voice was rough.

"I wanted to ask you some questions. About what you know about what happened between my great-great-grandfather and your grandfather."

The man looked at him then, his dark eyes serious. "You want to know what I think happened?"

"Yes."

"He wasn't of our blood. Our family. He married my grandmother. He was too fond of alcohol and card games. He lost a portion of the ranch playing cards with your great-great-grandfather. He was drunk and I think your great-great-grandfather was a cheat. There were witnesses that said he had an ace up his sleeve."

Chance nodded slowly. "And how is it… How is it you have the Sohappy name? If your grandfather wasn't part of the family."

The old man smiled. "I changed it back."

There was something in that simple statement that challenged a deeply held wall inside of Chance. Left it cracked.

That simple.

If something wasn't right, you changed it.

"Why are you asking now?" the old man asked, his eyes piercing. "Why now?"

"Because I realized just how wrong it is to hold on to your assumptions. When you could just ask. That's what we do, isn't it? We stay steeped in our own perspectives, and we never challenge them. We never looked to see what anyone went through. Juniper told me… She told me about something that happened at school. Someone who treated her badly because of her skin. I never saw anything like that. Not because it didn't happen, but because I wouldn't. Because people wouldn't do it in front of me, and they wouldn't do it to me. And you think then that that means things don't exist. Things you don't see. You think that your slice of the world is the whole thing, rather than just being a piece. I don't want to be like that anymore." He took a breath. "She has made me question a lot of things."

The old man's stare was sharp. "And now what will you do?"

"We need to redraw the boundary. We need to move the fence."

"Just like that?" he asked.

"Yes. Just like that."

"We should see if we can find proof."

He looked at the old man and saw pride radiating from him. And he knew he was never going to talk him out of that.

"All right. If that's what you want, then that's what we'll do."

He nodded.

"I had already agreed to see if my family had any records of what happened. I talked to Juniper about it."

"She's a good girl," her grandfather said. "She's going to make this place great."

"It looks to me like it's already pretty great. Because there's been a lot of great people here for a long time."

"It's family that helps make you who you are. But it seems to me that your great-grandfather, your grandfather… They didn't have an influence with you."

"Family does make you who you are," Chance said. "And sometimes, when what it would make is a bad thing, you have to make a decision to change it. My dad did that. I'm grateful to him. You have to break cycles or they just carry on. We need to break this cycle. We are neighbors. We don't need to hate each other."

Then the old man stuck his hand out, and Chance took it. And they shook.

Ten

"I heard that Chance had a conversation with Grandpa," Shelby said.

"What?" Juniper popped around the rack in the clothing store she and her sister were in.

"Yeah. Apparently, he came to get his side of the story. He told Dad about it, and Dad was floored. He couldn't believe it. He said he didn't think one of those, and I quote, *arrogant sons of bitches* would ever do something quite that reasonable."

"I… I don't even know what to say."

"You must be good in bed," Shelby said. Then she grinned.

"Don't say that out loud, and don't ever say it so Mom and Dad can hear you. Or Grandpa."

"Well, Grandpa has new respect for at least him.

So… Maybe things wouldn't be so bad if he found out."

"I have no desire for that to happen."

"Yeah. Fair. I mean, it would be somewhat horrifying."

"More than somewhat."

"So what exactly is going on with him? He must really like you to do that."

"I don't think so," Juniper said, suddenly feeling uncomfortable. "I think he's just… A lot nicer than I give him credit for. Or maybe *nice* is the wrong word. He's more reasonable. But there are things about him that I didn't know and…"

"Such as?"

"He… He had a sister that died. When she was really little. And he was just a kid and… I don't know. There's just more to him. There's sadness in him. And hearing him talk about his family, about the way that he loved her, it just made me feel…" She felt almost guilty telling Shelby about his pain, but…

If anyone understood loss, it was Shelby.

"Are you falling in love with him?"

She jerked up. "No. That would be impossible. Completely and utterly impossible. How would that even work?"

"I don't know. You seem to like him, plus you enjoy sleeping with him…"

"And that is not love," Juniper said.

"It's pretty close," Shelby responded. "Trust me."

"Surely there's more to it than that."

"Marriage is long. You have to find the person

that you like to be around most in the world. Who you most like to see naked."

Her sister smiled for a second, and then her smile dimmed. "Of course, marriage is long unless it isn't. I so forget sometimes."

"I'm sorry," Juniper said.

"Hey," Shelby said. "It's not your fault. And you don't need to keep yourself from being happy because of me."

Juniper laughed. "I'm not that benevolent."

"You actually are much more benevolent than you need to be. I mean, why are you in a feud with him to begin with? Why are you doing any of this?"

"What do you mean?"

"I'm just curious. What would you be doing if you didn't feel obligated to Grandpa?"

"I don't feel obligated," she said. "I agree with him about what's important. I care about it. I want to do the same things, because it matters to me."

"All right, I believe you. But I do wonder…"

"What do you wonder?"

"Are you keeping yourself from being really happy?"

Juniper frowned. "I don't understand."

"It's something I've been thinking a lot about," Shelby said. She got a faraway look in her eye.

"What?"

"How many things I do just because I'm already here. Just because I started doing something, and I don't know what else to do."

"I want to establish an equestrian program here

at the ranch. It's what I want to do, it's what I care about."

"But do you really care about border disputes and all of that, or is that just something that you're holding to because Grandpa was mad about it?"

"Those things matter. I'm not letting it go."

"At this point, what I wonder is if you're not letting it go because you feel more comfortable having that line drawn between yourself and Chance."

"I don't have any issues with Chance. Obviously."

"You lied to the man and kept him stowed away in your cabin when he got a head injury. And I feel like you do have some issues. With him, and maybe with relationships in general."

"I don't have issues with relationships."

"You're so dedicated to the land, Juniper. But why? At the exclusion of everything else? You wanted to do other things at one time…"

"But I realized I couldn't and still stay here and give it my all, and I needed to."

"Why is that? Is it because of Grandpa? Is it because you don't think Mom and Dad take his concern seriously enough? I know you love him, I know you have a really particular relationship with him. But it's not up to you to dedicate your whole life to this place. You can have the equestrian stuff without sacrificing everything else."

"I don't know how to do it. Anyway, I'm not in love with him, so it isn't an issue."

"Okay."

"Are you thinking about leaving?"

Shelby shook her head. "No. I'm not going to leave. But I'm thinking of going back to school. My life just isn't any of the things that I thought it would be. We were supposed to have kids, you know? And then that never happened, and I wish I would've done something, but we were just in a hurry to get married, and all I wanted was for us to have a family. Now he's gone too. That's the thing. He's gone too. And whatever I thought… It's not what I'm getting. It's not what I had. So, I need to figure out how to make something new. And thinking about that got me thinking about you. I don't know how you imagined your life at this point…"

"I didn't, really," she said. "I have the ranch. And that's what I care about."

"But you also have Chance."

"Stop saying that. I don't really have Chance. He's not… He's not a factor. He's just a dude. And he's not worth upending my life over. Good sex is hardly something to go crazy over."

"It's not nothing. Take it from someone who's been without for a good long while."

"Well. I appreciate the fact that you dreamed of that. Of the family and all of that. I just… I never did."

"Why not, Juniper?" she asked.

"Because you can't have everything, can you? You have to choose. You have to decide what manner of life you're going to make. And for me, the ranch is my primary baby."

"And who will you pass it on to?"

She looked at her sister, and she realized that right now… They were the last of the generation. The last of all the generations.

"I don't know. It doesn't matter. We'll be dead. So I won't care."

"It doesn't work like that. You don't care about generational legacy and then magically not care when you're old."

"Future Juniper's problem. I'll fuss about it when I'm a hundred."

"Well, I think you should worry about yourself a little bit now."

"Thank you for your feedback. I'll be sure to take that on board."

Shelby rolled her eyes and made a scoffing noise.

"What?"

"What is the point of even being your sister? You don't listen."

"You're the baby. It won't work. At least you tried."

"I did," Shelby said. She shook her head. "It wouldn't hurt you to try, you know?".

"I guess not."

Juniper grinned and went back to browsing.

The thing was, she heard what Shelby was saying. That Shelby didn't understand. She didn't want to do all this with the property. She didn't want to make the ranch her life. So, they were just different. They wanted different things.

And that was okay.

Juniper couldn't imagine a scenario wherein she

could make room in her life for a relationship that superseded the ranch. Shelby couldn't imagine a life where enjoying some hot sex with a good-looking man wouldn't end in love and marriage. That was fine. It was just the differences between the two of them. That was all.

There was nothing wrong with Juniper.

Nothing at all.

Eleven

He hadn't had dinner with his whole family for quite some time. But Callie was visiting from Gold Valley, and they had determined to have a dinner with all the siblings—except Buck—and their parents.

Dinner was loud and boisterous, as it always was when their family got together; it was just how they were.

"We need to talk for a second," he said, once everybody had dessert in front of them.

"What about?"

"I had a talk with Ron Sohappy," Chance said.

His dad scowled. "You mean he yelled at you and threatened to unleash his dogs on you?"

"No. I had a talk with him. About what happened initially with the ranch."

"And you think that he's going to tell you the truth?"

"I think he did, and I told him we'd try to find some sort of proof."

"How are we going to do that? Look for the smoking ace?"

Chance shook his head. "I've decided I don't want that. Why can't we share water rights? Why can't we work together? This feud has gone on long enough, and it's pointless. I want to be in a situation where I'm not fighting with my neighbor."

"That's noble of you, son," his dad said, "but I wonder what brought about the change of heart."

"It just seems like the right thing, Dad," Chance said. "And I care about it. I want us to do better than the generations that came before us, and I think we have. You know Grandpa was an asshole. Why are we on his side? Why do we listen to that story of how this ranch came to be, and how everything just is? I don't really understand. We have a chance to be better than those that came before us, and I believe that we need to do it. Because it's just right. Because it's fair."

"Hey, whatever you say, Chance, but I doubt you're ever going to join the two families together or anything like that," his dad said. "Some things are just too ingrained."

He nodded slowly. "I get that you feel that way. Because that's just how it's been. But I don't see why we gotta keep doing things one way just because it's how they've been."

"Well. If you say so."

"I do. Actually, I want to have them over for a barbecue."

"Damn," his dad said. "You really are trying to break ground."

His sister, Callie, smiled. "I like it, Chance," she said. "As you know, I'm all for shaking things up."

Being that she was responsible for the movement of women breaking into new events in the rodeo right now, he absolutely knew she'd understand.

"You're a good one, Callie," he said.

"I agree," said her husband, Jake.

"Well, I'll get planning," he said.

Of course, he was going to have to get Juniper to agree.

He wanted to make it right. He needed to. The journey they'd been on…

He felt suddenly like he was standing in front of old, familiar doors that were too forbidding to ever walk through.

They couldn't go on like this.

But he'd made his mind up.

And he could give her this.

"How good of a mood are you in?" he asked when she came through the door of his cabin that night.

She was no longer working at Evergreen Ranch; there was no need to keep up the pretense anymore. The fact of the matter was, he just wanted to spend time with her, and anyway, they just did when they wanted that.

"I don't understand how to answer that question," she said.

"Should I get you naked before I start asking you for things or…"

"Well, I'm always for being naked with you." She smiled.

It was the easy camaraderie between them that never failed to surprise him.

Because it was just there, and they didn't have to try, after all that time of sniping at each other for so long… This was just there.

They had way more in common than they had different. They both loved this place equally, and they were both willing to work to make it better.

They were both absolutely and completely stubborn, hardheaded pains in the ass. But they appreciated it about each other. So there was that.

"You better go ahead and pitch it now," she said, sighing heavily.

"I want to have a barbecue," he said. "With both of our families."

"What the hell?"

"I want to make some things clear. I don't want to fight with your family anymore. I want to fix it."

"Why?"

"Because it makes no earthly sense. All this bullshit. All this hanging on to things in the past. It doesn't make any sense."

"That's…" She sighed. "I mean, I guess you're

right. Honestly, I can't pretend that you're wrong. It's been a long time with all this stuff, and… I don't know that it benefits anyone."

"It doesn't. Your closest neighbors, and we should be allies, not enemies. We need to share the water rights."

"That's… I mean, it would definitely help."

"It would help us both. And I get that…that might seem like a bullshit thing to offer if your family was cheated." And he realized then, no matter what, there was only one real way this could go. "I want to sign the land back over to the Sohappy family. If you'll allow us water access, great. But it needs to go back to you. It's your land. Your blood."

Her eyes went glossy and he felt something terrible and fierce tighten his chest.

"I trust you," she said. "You don't need to sign the land over to us."

He felt like those words had cost her.

"You really are something," he said.

"Well, so are you. Something kind of undeniable, whether I want that to be true or not."

"It should be yours," he said, speaking of the land again.

She nodded. "Okay."

"So let's have a family barbecue. And let's put the bullshit feud to rest."

"I'd like that."

"I would like to get you naked also," he said, lowering his voice and moving toward her. And he kissed her, and it was like taking a full breath for the first time all day.

Because she was wonderful, brilliant. Amazing. Because she was everything that he had ever wanted.

Those words came out of nowhere and struck him like a thunderclap, and he chose not to pay them much mind. He chose not to think about them at all.

Instead, he just focused on her. On the way she looked, the way she tasted. He let the desire between them carry him somewhere else.

And it was like having amnesia again. Like being free of all the shit that weighed him down day in and day out. When they were together, it was like they both forgot.

And it was a gift. A blessing.

And he didn't normally use words like that or even think he needed them. But right now he would take them. Right now he would feel them.

But when she ran her hands over his skin, he tried to keep himself from feeling it too deeply.

When it was done, she curled up against him. "So when is this barbecue going to be?"

"I'd like to have it before my sister and her husband go back to Gold Valley. So as soon as possible."

"Well, my dad is retired, as he likes to remind me, so that means he's probably available whenever. Though, it'll be interesting to see if he will willingly sit in the same room as your dad. He doesn't feel the same way about the ranch that my grandpa does, but he's not neutral on the subject of the Carsons."

"We're going to do our best to change that. I don't want them to be neutral. I want him to actually have some nice feelings for us. Let's be neighborly."

"You and I might be someplace past neighborly," she said.

"Yeah, maybe." He moved over top of her and kissed her. "Spend the night with me."

She nodded. "Okay."

But for the rest of the night there was no need for talking.

It hadn't been easy to convince her family to come to a barbecue hosted by the Carsons. And, of course, her grandmother had refused to go empty-handed, so that meant a rally to make mass amounts of fry bread.

And keeping it hot on the drive over was everyone's burden.

Juniper, Shelby, their mother and father and their grandparents all drove separate trucks over to the ranch. And when they pulled up to the grand main house at Evergreen Ranch, Juniper knew a moment of disquiet.

The Carsons were something else. They were wealthy, they were extravagant with it even, and her family had a much more modest existence.

But when Chance broke away from his brothers and his parents to come and greet them, she felt some of her disquiet dissipate. She just hoped that her family didn't see the connection between the two of them.

Because that was something she didn't want to have to explain on top of everything else.

But he was so… Oh, he was wonderful and she couldn't keep the smile off her face. The way he spoke to her parents, her grandfather and grandmother. The respect and manners, and she really didn't know that would make her swoon, but it did.

Her family mattered.

And he was treating them exactly as she wanted them to be treated.

"Thank you for coming," he said. "We really appreciate it." He shook her grandfather's hand first. Then went to her grandmother.

After that, he greeted her parents.

Then he moved to Shelby, who treated him to a sly look. "You must be Shelby," he said. "Haven't seen you in a while."

"No. Neither. Except I did see you from a distance a few weeks ago."

"I see."

"Yeah," she said.

Juniper elbowed her.

"What?" she asked.

The brothers all took their turns making introductions, and then they all got to setting out food.

Her grandfather, who wasn't shy at all, immediately engaged the senior Carson.

"Your son is a good man," he said.

Abe Carson nodded. "He is."

They talked about cows, they talked about water, they talked about the rodeo.

Once the rodeo stories started, they didn't stop.

At the big table, which was laden down with meat, and her grandmother's fry bread, she was seated next to Callie, Chance's sister.

"Hi," she said. "I know who you are, but I don't think we've ever really met."

Callie was bright and chipper, and she made Juniper feel old. But then, she had to be somewhere around five years older than her.

"Yeah. It's good to see you."

"I think it's great what Chance is doing. That he cares about getting everybody together, and making sure they're getting along."

"Yeah. I never would've thought it about him, but he seems invested in it."

"He seems to like you," she said.

And Juniper stiffened. She wasn't sure how anyone could get that from their interactions.

"Does he?"

She shrugged. "Just a feeling I get. When he looks at you."

"Oh. Well. He's a good guy. He really is."

"I think so."

At some point, half the people bundled up and went to target practice, and everybody ended up out by the gravel pit on the property, sitting in lawn chairs and drinking beers and shooting rifles.

And there was a time when she would've worried about her grandfather having a rifle around the Carsons, but things seemed to be just... Different now. Was it all because of the way that Chance had gone to talk to Grandpa?

Had it really been enough to change the tone of the relationship between their families?

Maybe respect was the first, most important step. And then listening.

It forced her to see him differently, watching this interaction with his family.

Yet again.

And what she couldn't quite believe was the way that things had changed between them in these past weeks. The way that her ideas had been challenged.

When she went back home, her dad commented how they were actually such a nice family.

And she didn't... She didn't know what to do about that.

All of a sudden this barrier had been lifted, one that had once existed between herself and Chance. And yes, it could be argued that that had been dispensed with the minute they started sleeping together, but that had been something else. And this was... This was something emotional, and she didn't quite know what to do with it.

"Thank you," her grandfather said. "Your commitment to the ranch is truly commendable. I feel like you must've done something to make him change the way that he saw things."

Oh, that made her feel terrible.

Because it had been so momentous for her to be given the chance to run the ranch, and it meant the world to her to do right by her opportunity.

But what would they think if they found out that a huge reason Chance had changed his mind about everything was because she'd slept with him? Even if that was a simplified version of events, it was how it would look. Like she'd bought the land back with her body. By sleeping with the enemy.

"I just care about the ranch," she said. "It's my life, Grandpa, you know that."

He nodded his head. "I know."

"I'll honor it."

"I know," he said again. He patted her hand. "You're a good girl."

There. She was a good girl.

That was everything she had ever wanted to be. And now that she had it, she didn't know quite what to make of it.

Except… She really had no reason to continue on being with Chance.

And it wasn't sad or anything like that. There was no reason for it to be. They were at a conclusion. She was actually really happy. It might've all happened in a strange roundabout way, but she had accomplished something. She had changed some things. For the better. And she was just so grateful for that. Because they didn't need each other anymore.

And they didn't hate each other. And surely that was progress. Surely.

"Good night," she said, giving her grandpa a half wave.

"Good night."

And then she went back to her cabin and went to bed alone, and tried to tell herself that it was just fine.

Twelve

Juniper went down to the First Bank of Lone Rock the very next day. She was ready to try to get her loan to get the barn built.

A newer barn. A bigger one.

Yes, she would continue to work on restoring the one that she and Chance had worked on together, but she wanted something state-of-the-art, cutting-edge. She had her money saved up for the first of her horses, and this, she would be getting some help on.

Her plan was also to rent out space for people to board their horses, helping turn more of a profit at the ranch.

So a state-of-the-art facility was important.

And she finally had all of the years at her job required to go for a loan this size.

It was a big deal. Because this was debt. Real debt. Attached to her name. This was all the real stuff, as real as it got, in fact. This was her marriage. Her dream.

She laughed hollowly.

Then she walked into the banker's office, and two hours later, she was fully approved for the loan.

Now she would just need to line up construction workers and all of that. She had her plans, which she had needed before she could present them to the bank.

It felt big. And the first thing she wanted to do was… Call Chance.

She didn't need to. He wasn't a key part of this enterprise or anything like that. He wasn't even a factor.

She could call Shelby, and she did want to talk to Shelby about it. But she found she wanted to share the triumph with him, and she didn't quite know what to do with that.

They didn't talk on the phone, not very often. Mostly it was just texts back and forth. And then they were together. To hook up, not anything else. They'd never been on a date. Of course, when you had held a man captive while he had amnesia, she supposed you didn't really need to go on a date.

That was just kind of silly.

"Stupid," she muttered, and took her phone out, and found Chance's name in her messages.

"Hey," he said. "Everything okay?"

"Everything is wonderful," she said. "I got a loan. I'm building a new equestrian facility."

"That's… That's good. You want to do that, right?"

"Yes," she said. "I do. I really do. Chance, this is the biggest… It's the biggest thing. Nothing else has ever been this big."

"We should go out and celebrate," he said.

And her heart swooped inside of her chest. "Really?"

"Yes. We should. We should go out and celebrate that you're amazing."

"I… Okay."

And that was how she found herself at Shelby's. "He wants to go out," she said.

"You've been sleeping with the guy for like a month."

She nodded. And she didn't tell Shelby that she had just been thinking about how she needed to end things with him. About how she needed the two of them to get back to some semblance of sanity.

Because all that they were was a little bit intense.

Because there was no point. Because they had that whole reconciliation with the family, and her whole goal of having him see her and her family as people had been realized.

"And you need a dress," Shelby said.

"It's dumb, right? That I would want to wear a dress for a man?"

"It's not dumb," Shelby said. "It's normal. I know you don't have a lot of experience with this…"

"Well. It's because I… I've been trying so hard

to live up to the fact that I'm the first girl to get this opportunity."

"Juniper," Shelby said. "That's ridiculous. Grandpa doesn't care that you're not a boy."

"No. And he totally thinks I can do anything that a boy could do. That isn't what I mean, it's just… I'm the first. And our great-great-grandpa who lost the ranch was the first to not be part of the family by blood and make a mistake and…and then it was why Grandpa didn't want Chuck to have the ranch. Why he wanted it in the family. So I can assume if I screw up…"

"First of all," Shelby said, "you'll be in charge. So you'll get to decide who carries it all on. Second, he wouldn't have given it to Chuck. Not ever. He'd have always trusted you with it, no matter the family history."

"But…"

"And if you have to love this land more than everything else, who will you pass it to?"

"I was counting on you reproducing."

Shelby laughed. "Well, that's blown to hell, isn't it? You might have to make your own life." Her tone softened. "You have to do what you want, you can't just be the fulfillment of Grandpa's dreams. He isn't going to live that much longer, Juniper. He's ninety-four."

"He could live another ten years," Juniper said. And it made her feel panicky, because she really did love him more than just about anyone or anything else.

"I know that you love him," Shelby said. "And I know that all of this comes from how much you love him. But he wants you to be happy. You didn't ever have to be a boy. You didn't ever have to love nothing more than this ranch."

She did her best not to let her sister's words sink too deep. "I still don't own a dress. And I would like to wear one to go out with Chance."

"Well, I can accommodate you. Especially because my dresses don't get any use these days."

Her sister tried to smile, but it came out a little bit thin.

She grabbed a stack of dresses, and after she had tried on two, Juniper suddenly understood why women were often upset about the shapes of their bodies.

Some of them showed off too much of her hips, some of them were too low-cut. And some of them emphasized that she had a little bit of roundness to her stomach.

"These are instruments of torture. Mental torture," she said.

"It's fine," Shelby said. "Wear the red one. You look amazing in it."

"What if I'm wrong?" she said, staring at her reflection. "What if he just wants to go to a bar and have a beer? Like friends?"

"Well, you'll be the best-looking bitch in the bar."

"Oh no, I'll feel really stupid. What if I have all of this wrong?"

"I thought you didn't want it to turn into anything."

"I don't," she said, her heart pounding heavily. "I don't want it to be anything else. I want it to be… What it is. I actually wanted it to be over." She was always meaning to not tell her sister things, and then accidentally blurting them out.

"You wanted it to be over?" Shelby asked, her eyes wide.

"Yes. I just wanted things to get back to normal. Or, not normal, better. Because I did it, right? I mean, I showed Grandpa that the Carsons could be good people, and I showed Chance that we weren't wrong about the situation with the land and how it wasn't fair. I did that. So, the two of us don't need to be together anymore."

"Did you stop being attracted to him?"

"No. Not at all. He's gorgeous…"

"I know," she said. "I've seen him."

"He's gorgeous, and I like being around him… And don't say anything. It's not that, it's just that today when I got the loan I just wanted to talk to him."

"You care about him," Shelby said.

"I like him. And I don't know what to do with that. I've never split my focus from the ranch. I do the EMT thing because it's necessary, and it was… Look, it wasn't really being a doctor, but it helped with the ranch instead of taking from it. I needed it for the money. But I need to love the ranch more than I love anything else. It needs to be the thing that I focus on, it needs to be…"

"You're a human being," Shelby said. "And it doesn't matter whether you were born you or born a man. You're just you. And you get to be a human being."

"I don't know how. I don't know how to have balance. I don't know how to have… Any of this. All I know is the ranch, all I know is obsession."

"Maybe this is a great opportunity to try and not just be obsessed. With him or the ranch."

"I guess. Do you have lipstick? Who am I?"

"You're my sister," Shelby said. "And will figure this out."

Thirteen

He pulled into Juniper's driveway at five, because while she had asked if they could meet in town, he had decided that was bullshit, and he needed to take her, since they were celebrating something, and... Hell. He just wanted to. He couldn't recall the last time he had felt compelled to take a woman out, and in fact, he wasn't sure he ever had.

Maybe this was the chance to...finish it.

Not that he was going to end things tonight, but it might be a good chance to draw a line under things.

The issues with the family were resolved.

Maybe this would tie up the unfinished business with them.

Maybe you just want to be with her...

He shrugged that off.

And then when she came out of the house, his stomach went tight. She was beautiful in a red dress that hugged her figure and stopped just above her knee. She had on red lipstick, her black hair loose and hanging around her shoulders.

He had never seen her look quite so… She was always beautiful. He didn't care what she wore. She was the damn sexiest woman he had ever seen. That was just a fact. But right now she was testing him. Testing the limits of his restraint.

He got out of the truck and rounded to her side, opening the door for her. She looked up at him, her dark eyes wide. "What…"

And then he leaned in and kissed her. Hard.

"You look beautiful."

Her face went scarlet. "Thank you."

"No problem."

It was a bit of a drive down into Lone Rock, and he had been thinking of taking her to the Thirsty Mule, but he was going to have to take her to the Horseshoe. The old saloon building was restored to its original glory, with luxurious private dining rooms, and all kinds of things that hearkened back to the Gold Rush era of Lone Rock.

It was a favorite of his family, and they ate there every Christmas Eve.

"You like the food here?"

"There aren't many options in town," she said.

It was true. Lone Rock was tiny, a little gold speck out in Eastern Oregon, with very little surrounding it. The main street of the town was all original buildings, restored over the years to keep the look of the late 1800s alive.

It was certainly never going to modernize.

"Well, it is the best food in town," he said. "But don't tell Cara I said that, or she'll start a riot."

"The food at the Mule's great," she said. "It's just that, you know, it's…"

"Bar food?"

"Yes."

"You've never really lived anywhere else, have you?" he asked.

"No," she said.

"I have," he said.

"Where all have you lived?"

"Well, if I'm honest, mostly in an RV in different locations." They got out of the truck and walked toward the restaurant. "You know, until we had to slow down for Sophie. The nearest hospital. We lived on the outskirts of Portland for quite a while. Sophie needed to be near Doernbecher so she could receive specialized care. The Children's Hospital there is one of the best in the country."

"Oh wow. That must've been very different."

"It was. But… We were willing to do anything for her health. And then after that… Well, my grandpa died, and Lone Rock seemed like the place to go. With Evergreen Ranch available, that was just where we went. It was the best thing. For all of us."

They walked inside the restaurant, and Janine, the hostess, who he'd known since he was a kid, greeted them.

"Your usual table?"

His family often rented private dining.

"It's just the two of us tonight," he said. "We can sit out in the main dining area."

The carpets were a rich cranberry color, with the original lights, covered in carnival glass, turned low to give the place a romantic ambience. The tables were covered in white tablecloths, the walls red brick.

"I've actually never eaten here," Juniper said when they took a seat.

"Never?"

"It's not really our…"

"Hey. I get it. We're from different experiences."

"Well, I appreciate that you understand that."

"I do. I more than understand it."

He decided to go for an expensive bottle of champagne, in spite of her protests, and encouraged her to order exactly what she wanted, no matter what the cost was. She gave him a slightly wicked look. "I have always wanted to pretend like ordering something expensive meant I was afraid I'd have to pay for it with my body."

"I am happy to accommodate that fantasy," he said, his voice getting gravelly.

She ordered the fillet.

He gave thanks.

He loved watching her eat. Loved watching her smile and sigh over every bite. And he encouraged her to order a couple of different desserts after they brought out the tray with all the examples of the evening's selections.

"You can take the extras home," he said. "But it really is the best."

After much pushing, she agreed.

When they were finally finished, he had several boxes for her to take back home with her.

And he liked that. He liked giving her things. He liked seeing her happy. And he couldn't remember the last time he'd ever felt like that. Like sharing in somebody else's enjoyment was as good as having his own.

"Why don't you come back to my place?" she asked.

And he wasn't going to argue.

Something felt different between them tonight, and she didn't know if it was the dress or the dinner. She just didn't know. She felt different.

And she was… Electrified with it.

All the way back to the tiny cabin, she let herself get more and more wound up. She wanted him so badly she could hardly stand it. Maybe it was the adrenaline rush of having him again when she had been determined to break it off and never experience the pleasure of his hands on her skin. Maybe it was that she wanted him in a way that made her entire body ache. In a way that made her feel like he had been worth the wait, even though she would've said that she wasn't waiting for him. And tonight she felt completely and utterly one with her womanhood, and that was another thing she had struggled with. Even with him. Even as he had made her feel like her curves were a good thing. Like her body was special. Wonderful. Valuable. She couldn't say that she had felt purely feminine, or purely comfortable with it. But something about the dress, that lipstick, the whole night, made her feel a connection with herself that she hadn't before.

They got out of the truck, and her hands were shaking as they went up the front steps into the house. Then she turned and launched herself into his arms. She kissed him like she was dying, parted her lips and let him consume her.

And he did.

"I hope you know you don't actually have to pay for the steak," he said.

She laughed. "Maybe I just like the fantasy?"

"Do you?"

"Because I never felt like I was one of the pretty girls. Because I never felt like I was allowed to be. Because I never… Because always for me it's been about being convenient, not caught up in passion."

"I want you," he said. "You. This has nothing to do with feuds or anything else. I just want you."

"Thank you," she breathed, and she kissed him again, pouring all of her desire, all of her passion, into it.

He moved his hand around her back and unzipped her dress, leaving her in the borrowed high heels she was wearing and her underwear, leaving her feeling more feminine than she ever had in her life.

She stood back, leaning against the wall and arching her hips forward. He growled, pressing his hand to the front of his jeans, to where he was already hard and in desperate need of her.

"You want this?"

She nodded.

Then she went over to him and put her hands on his chest, slid them down his body as she dropped to her knees.

She had never done this before. Because she had never been in a relationship long enough to think that the man merited this kind of special treatment, and she knew that some women treated it like a free and easy thing. A little bit of action without the commitment of full-on sex, but she had always felt like there was something a bit more intimate about it, and she had always hesitated to try it.

But not with him. Not with him at all.

She undid his belt buckle, undid the zipper on his jeans and freed him, wrapping her hand around his heavy arousal, looking up at him as she leaned in and stroked him from base to head with the tip of her tongue.

His breath hissed through his teeth, the glint of desire in his eyes nearly undoing her completely. She felt powerful. Female. Incredible.

She took him into her mouth, as deep as she could, and began to suck him like he was her favorite flavor of Popsicle. The taste of him was… Amazing. And she would never have thought that. But then, she thought he was singularly beautiful. She could write poetry about his anatomy, without ever having been all that impressed with the look of a naked man before this.

But she loved the look of him.

He was glorious. The most incredible man she had ever seen in her life. And she reveled in just what she was making him feel now. What she alone seemed to be able to make him feel. If there was anyone else, she didn't want to know about the bitch. She wanted to be the only one.

It made her feel desperately sad that she wasn't… That she couldn't be… That it couldn't be forever.

Why not?

Because it couldn't be. It couldn't be so easy.

And to just decide that you wanted forever when, before, you didn't think you did. To just decide that you loved a man when, before, he was your sworn enemy. To be able to love something more than her family land when she'd committed to not allowing herself that. Not ever.

It couldn't be that easy.

She shut her brain down and continued to lick, suck and stroke his masculine body.

She brought him to the brink, until his thigh muscles were shaking, and then he grabbed hold of her hair and moved her away from him, nearly lifting her up off the ground by her hair and bringing her in to kiss him. "I have to have you," he growled.

"No complaints from me," she said breathlessly. He lifted her against him and kissed her. Wildly. Recklessly. Then he carried her back into the bedroom, and she stopped him, pulling him up against her, pulling them both against the wall.

"Is that how you want it?" he growled.

"Yes," she whispered.

He pulled her panties aside, pushing his fingers between her legs, then dropping to his knees, taking her with his mouth, putting her thighs over his shoulders and eating her diligently as he pinned her body against the wall.

She arched against it, pushing her hips more firmly against his mouth as he continued to consume her.

She dug her fingers into his shoulders, tugged at his hair.

"Please," she begged. "Please."

"Not until you come for me," he said.

His words, electric, magic, set off a spark inside of her body that started deep within, shivering outward as it bloomed into a deep, endless climax that left her gasping. Left her breathless.

Then he rose up and, keeping her pinned against the wall, thrust into her, her hands pressed back against the drywall, held firmly in place by his ironclad grip, as he thrust, hard and fast, into her body. And it was a funny thing, because this was how she had always thought it would be between them. Desperate and needy, and not with the civility of a bed.

But their first time had been in a bed, and now here they were against that wall, when there was no more hate between them. When there was no more distrust.

But they had made it here. And somehow, something in her had always known they would.

She had always known that they would. And as her eyes met his, she knew why.

Because she loved him. She felt it clear and loud inside of her. She loved him.

She loved Chance Carson, and it didn't matter if it felt impossible. Because she would do whatever it took for the two of them to be together.

She wasn't only a rancher.

She didn't only love this ranch. She didn't only love her family name. She loved him. And it felt like a powerful realization. One that made her feel like she could scarcely breathe. Scarcely think.

He thrust into her, and her climax hit her like a wave, and then his own overtook him just a split second later, like a lightning bolt had gone through them both at once.

He held her while he shook, while he spent himself inside of her, and she clung to him. And she knew.

She knew. She had no idea what he would say. No idea what he would do. But it was the truth, and she could no more keep it in than she could ever keep in the animosity that she had once felt for him.

Because above all else, between herself and Chance Carson, there wasn't room for any more lying.

She had lied to him once already, and she would never do it again. "I'm sorry," she said, stroking his hair, and she hadn't meant to say that. Hadn't meant to say that she was sorry, but it had come out, and she realized once it did that it had been an important thing for her to say. "I should never have lied to you. When I found you. I should've taken you straight back to your family. I'm so sorry that I did that. It was selfish. I was blinded by the fact that the only thing that I thought mattered was the ranch, was getting even, was getting what I wanted. I wanted to force you to see something... And it was wrong of me. I swear I will never lie to you. Not again."

"It's okay," he said, looking slightly mystified by her intensity.

But he would understand. Eventually, he would understand.

"And the thing is," she said, touching his face, "I love you, Chance Carson. And I need you to believe me. I need you to trust me. I love you, Chance, and I would be willing to do anything, absolutely anything, to get you to love me back. Because I've never wanted anything but this ranch, and now that I've committed myself to it, now that I'm in debt for it, all of that... Now that I have that, what I want more is you. But it's a good thing. I want you. And I will split my time anywhere. And I said I'd never do that. But I would. For you. For you I would."

"Juniper," he said, his voice rough.

"You don't have to say anything," she said. "You don't have to say anything now. It's just... I'm kind of blown away by how strong I feel about this. By the fact that for the first time... For the first time I know what I want. Not what someone else wants for me. And not what I think I have to do. Just what I want.

So. It's okay if you can't feel the same. It's okay if you can't answer me yet. I'm just glad that I know. I'm glad that I know." But her mouth was dry, and her whole body felt like it was poised on the edge of a knife, and it did matter. It did fucking matter what he said. What he wanted. It mattered because if he didn't want her... Well, if he didn't want her, then everything was just going to be kind of terrible.

"Juniper, I..."

"You're going to say something anyway. You hardheaded asshole."

"I'm not going to leave you thinking that I might be able to... That I might change my mind. That I might change who I am. I won't. I can't."

"You're right about one part. You won't."

"You don't understand..."

"I understand what it's like to live your whole life so afraid that you're going to do the wrong thing, and then the person that you love most in the world will tell you that you want what they wanted. I know that fear. But you know what, if that's how my grandfather feels, then that's how he feels. And if that's how you feel... That's the thing, I can't control what anyone else feels. I can't control what you say or do or want. I can only control myself. I love you." She swallowed hard, tears springing into her eyes, and normally, she would despise that weakness. But right now she couldn't. Right now she didn't.

Right now all that mattered was she knew how she felt. And she wasn't afraid. She felt more herself than she ever had. She felt like... She didn't need to perform. She didn't need to do anything but be. And this was who she was. She loved the ranch, and she wouldn't compromise. She loved Chance, and she wouldn't compromise there either.

This was the most vulnerable she'd ever been, but also the most certain. And as difficult as she could feel the coming moment would be, she didn't resent it. Because it had brought her to this place of being one with herself. Certain of herself.

"Juniper, this isn't what I want. I watched my parents' lives be torn apart by losing a child, and I... I lost my sister. And I can't... I can't."

It broke her. But she wasn't angry.

She had been angry with this man so many times over things that weren't justified, and she had a feeling she would be a little bit justified in being angry about this. But she wasn't. She just wasn't.

Because she could see that he believed it. Deep down in his soul, and she understood that. She knew what it was to believe something so deeply about yourself.

It was all fear. That was what it was. Fear of losing the thing that you had, all that you had managed to make for yourself, in exchange for something that felt uncertain. Something you had lived without all this time, so maybe you didn't even actually want it, maybe you didn't need it.

"I want you to remember something," she said. "That I loved you. Even when you said you couldn't. That I care about you. I want you to remember that."

"Juniper..."

"No. I don't want your apologies. I don't want your speeches. You know what you can and can't do. You know who you are. And if you don't, I hope you find out. And then I hope you come find me. But if not, I want you to know... I think we really could've been something. Something I didn't even think I believed in. But now here I am, asking for it. Demanding it."

"I can't."

"Then you have to let me go," she said.

And she looked at him, and realized his face had become the dearest thing in the world to her, and it hurt to walk away. It hurt worse than anything ever had. Than she'd imagined anything ever could.

But she would let him go anyway.

Because she wouldn't compromise. And she finally realized she didn't have to.

Because she didn't need to be in service to what her grandfather wanted in order to be loved. Any more than she needed to leave the ranch to love Chance. Any more than she needed to keep her feelings to herself, or to stand there and compromise.

She had meant it when she'd said she didn't need him to say anything now. It was true.

But if he insisted on ending this, she would accept it. And she felt... Impossibly brave making that choice. To speak her heart to the person she loved most in the world and risk losing him.

And he left.

And her home felt empty, and so did she.

She sat in her pain for a long time, tried to sleep

and failed. Marinated in her pain all day the next day until she finally drove from her cabin, to her grandfather's house. Her heart in pieces.

She walked up the steps and went inside, her heart thundering heavily. "Juniper," he said when he saw her. "What brings you here?"

"I have something to tell you."

"Yes?"

"I'm in love with a Carson. And I love the ranch. And I love you. I'm not a son, and I'm sorry. I'm a granddaughter. But I love this place, and I will take care of it. I'll take care of it even if I end up living at Evergreen Ranch. I'll take care of it if Chance doesn't love me back and rejects me. And I'll love you even if that makes you angry. But I need you to know. I need you to understand."

"Juniper," her grandfather said, his voice rough. "You thought that I wouldn't love you?"

"It isn't that. But I promised you I'd do this. Perfectly. And I was just so afraid… I was just so afraid. That I couldn't quite be what you wanted. That I wasn't quite what you needed. And I wanted to prove myself. I gave up on my dreams of medical school. Of being a doctor. I threw myself into everything I could do here. All this time. And the problem is I liked Chance, from the first moment I saw him, and I wanted to hate him with the fire of a thousand suns, so I did everything I could to make that happen. But I didn't. I've always wanted him."

"I never wanted you to not be true to yourself," her grandfather said. "Not ever. I love you, and I want you to be happy. I'm sorry if an old grudge made you feel that you had to do anything differently."

Juniper laughed, but she wasn't mad. She wasn't. The risk had been hers to take all along, to be honest about herself and who she was, and she hadn't taken it.

And now she had taken the risk, she had spoken her truth. She had faced down her fears, with Chance, and now with her grandfather. And she might've lost Chance for now, but her grandfather was looking at her with love, and she knew that she'd made the right choice. She knew that things would be okay. They would be.

"Juniper," her grandmother said. "Will you stay for dinner?"

She could wait to dissolve. She would dissolve. Because she wanted Chance, and right now, he didn't want her. Or at least, he didn't think he could.

"Yes," she said. "I will."

Because there would always be time for her to dissolve. Because the grief would be waiting for her when she got up from this table.

But right now she had her grandparents. She had her family. And she had herself. And she would take a moment to celebrate that.

Fourteen

He couldn't sleep. Or worse, he could. And when he did, he dreamed. And he was back there. Standing in front of the hospital, unable to go through the doors.

Because whatever was behind there was so terrible he couldn't face it.

He couldn't bring himself to stand. Couldn't bring himself to move over there. He was completely blocked. Bound by an invisible force that he couldn't see. That made it impossible to breathe.

Grief. His body whispered the truth of it even as his brain resisted giving it a name. Grief.

So much grief, and his feet felt like they were encased in cement. And he couldn't take a single step.

His breathing was labored, and when he did finally wake up, he was in a cold sweat.

Grief. This unending grief.

But it wasn't Sophie he was thinking of. It was Juniper.

He had really told her that he couldn't do it. That he couldn't love her.

You already do.

Maybe that was true. But how? He didn't understand.

He felt like she was there, just on the other side of that door, but for some reason, for some damned reason, he couldn't get there. He didn't understand it. He didn't know how the hell to make sense of it. He wished that there was someone he could talk to, but he found he only wanted to talk to Juniper.

And he had sent her away, so, that was going to work out real well for him.

He loved her. It was the reason he had been motivated to talk to her grandfather. The reason he'd wanted to bring the families together for a barbecue. And he knew that he did. He knew that rejecting her was cowardice.

But what had he been thinking? That she wouldn't want it to be love? That it wouldn't come down to this? Of course it had. It was inevitable. It had always been fucking inevitable between the two of them. There had never been any other option. And yet he was running scared of it. Running scared of it like a child, not acting at all like a man.

Why can't you go through the damned hospital doors? And it took a while to realize he'd said it out loud. Why couldn't he go?

He had regretted it. All of this time he had regretted it, and here he was, doing it to himself again. Ruining things for himself again.

You will regret it always if you don't do it. That's all you have to do. Just have the balls to move forward.

It was the hardest thing. But this was different than having his sister behind those doors, dying, with no chance of survival.

This was an unknown. And maybe on the other side there would be joy. Maybe there would be struggle. Maybe there would be pain. But it would be worth it. It would be worth it.

For her. And suddenly that made all the difference. Imagining her walking forward with him. Imagining her there, taking his hand and leading him through.

And yeah, all the bullshit he'd ever had to deal with was right there still. Behind those doors.

But so was the potential for everything else. For joy, for love, for happiness. The kind that he had let himself believe he didn't want, let alone need.

But he did.

And most of all, he needed her.

Walking with him.

But he had to take that first step on his own.

He got out of bed, and then Chance Carson took a step forward.

* * *

Juniper was out working when Chance showed up.

She recognized the sound of his truck now. Recognized him.

Just the feel of him.

It was because she was different now. Because they were different.

She dropped the stack of wood she was holding and stood there, watching as he crossed the space and made his way to her.

"What are you doing here?"

"I walked through the door," he said. "And I'm ready. For whatever's on the other side of it. I'm ready. I recognize that it's been what's holding me back. I punished myself for all those years, for not being able to go and see my sister one last time. And I felt like it meant I wasn't going to be able to go any kind of distance for anyone. I felt like I deserved to sit in that same loneliness she might've felt because I wasn't there. But you know what, that's self-protective bullshit. It was never about me. That's the thing. It never was. It's always just been about love. I loved her, and I was a kid, and it kept me frozen. Loving you kept me frozen too. But I remember what it was like to forget. To forget that I'd ever been hurt, to look at you without any of that weighing me down, and it made me want to change."

His breath was unsteady and it made her heart seize up, but he kept on talking. "It makes me want to reach out. Makes me want to walk through the door. Because there I was, when you walked away, standing on the outside just like I was then. I don't want that. I don't want to stand on the outside anymore. I don't just want to be looking in. I want to be with you. Even if it hurts. I want to be with you no matter what's on the road ahead of us. For a while I got to forget. And that was a powerful thing. But it's so much more powerful to stand here remembering all of it. Every fight we've had, every shitty thing I've been through, and want to be with you anyway. Because I do. Please believe that. It just took me a long while to realize.

"Juniper, I know how much it hurts to lose somebody. I've held it close for all these years. But I almost chose to lose you, and I can't accept that. I can't accept that choice I nearly made. Because it isn't living. When I have all this, when I have you, standing there wanting me, how can I choose any different? How can I choose not to love you when I already do? How can I choose to walk away like it would be the best thing? It wouldn't be. It wouldn't be living. Yes, I'm living with grief, but I'm still living. And so many people are, so many people do, every day, and they still choose to love. My parents chose to keep on loving. They had another child, even after all that. It's the lesson I missed. That love is worth it. Every time. No matter what. Love is always worth it."

"I love you," she said, flinging her arms around his neck, her heart pounding heavily.

"I love you too," he whispered, his breath hot against her ear.

And she wept. She thought maybe he did too. "We can live here," he said, his voice rough. "Whatever you want."

"Really?"

"Yes. We can live here. We can live in Evergreen Ranch. Hell, we can live at both. Or away. You could go to medical school. Be a doctor like you wanted. Stay here, make the equestrian thing happen. Do both. Do everything. Do nothing. Just be with me, and I'll be with you."

He was so earnest, so…him. The man she'd rescued, who had no memory. The man who'd had it all come blazing back. He was both.

And he was willing to give up the thing that stood between them: the land.

And she realized in that moment she was too.

"You would live here, in my tiny little house?" she asked.

"Home is wherever you are. Love is where you are. I… I only just realized… I didn't need to be in the hospital. Because my love was there already. Love goes before you. And it always goes with you. It's not a place. And for me, it's you."

"For me, it's you."

"You said you couldn't compromise."

"Well, that was back when I would've told you I couldn't have loved a Carson."

"And when was that?"

She smiled. "You know what, I can't remember. Maybe I have amnesia."

"As long as you never forget how much you love me."

"Oh, Chance, I could never forget that."

"Do you still want me to be your ranch hand?"

"I wouldn't say no."

"What if I was just your husband?"

"I can't imagine what our grandfathers would say about a Carson and a Sohappy getting married."

"It doesn't matter what they would say," Chance said, grinning.

And she smiled, because it was true. "You know, all that really matters is that we want it."

"And I do."

"I do too."

She kissed him, and she could only ever marvel about the fact that she loved him now far more than she had ever hated him. And one thing she knew for sure, it wasn't his ranch or hers that would be their greatest legacy.

It was love.

It was the only thing that had ever made their land worth anything. Love.

And it was the thing that made life worth living.

Always and forever.

* * * * *

Look for the next book in
The Carsons of Lone Rock series, coming soon.
And if you can't get enough Maisey Yates,
check out her Gold Valley Vineyards series
from Harlequin Desire.

Rancher's Wild Secret
Claiming the Rancher's Heir
The Rancher's Wager
Rancher's Christmas Storm

WE HOPE YOU ENJOYED
THIS BOOK FROM

✦ HARLEQUIN
DESIRE

*Luxury, scandal, desire—welcome to
the lives of the American elite.*

Be transported to the worlds of oil barons, family dynasties,
moguls and celebrities. Get ready for juicy plot twists,
delicious sensuality and intriguing scandal.

6 NEW BOOKS AVAILABLE EVERY MONTH!

HDHALO2021

COMING NEXT MONTH FROM

DESIRE

#2857 THE REBEL'S RETURN
Texas Cattleman's Club: Fathers and Sons • by Nadine Gonzalez
Eve Martin has one goal—find her nephew's father—and her unlikely ally is hotelier Rafael Wentworth, who's just returned to Texas and the family who abandoned him. Soon she's falling hard for the playboy in spite of their differences...and their secrets.

#2858 SECRETS OF A BAD REPUTATION
Dynasties: DNA Dilemma • by Joss Wood
Musician Griff O'Hare uses his bad-boy persona to keep others at bay. But when he's booked by straitlaced Kinga Ryder-White for her family's gala, he can't ignore their attraction. Yet as they fall for one another, everything around them falls apart...

#2859 HUSBAND IN NAME ONLY
Gambling Men • by Barbara Dunlop
Everyone believes ambitious Adeline Cambridge and rugged Alaskan politician Joe Breckenridge make a good match. So after one unexpected night and a baby on the way, their families push them into marriage. But will the convenient arrangement withstand the sparks and secrets between them?

#2860 EVER AFTER EXES
Titans of Tech • by Susannah Erwin
Dating app creator Will Taylor makes happily-ever-afters but remains a bachelor after his heart was broken by Finley Smythe. Reunited at a remote resort, they strike an uneasy truce after being stranded together. The attraction's still there even as their complicated past threatens everything...

#2861 ONE NIGHT CONSEQUENCE
Clashing Birthrights • by Yvonne Lindsay
As the widow of his best friend, Stevie Nickerson should be off-limits to CEO Fletcher Richmond, but there's a spark neither can ignore. When he learns she's pregnant, he insists on marriage, but Stevie relishes her independence. Can the two make it work?

#2862 THE WEDDING DARE
Destination Wedding • by Katherine Garbera
After learning a life-shattering secret, entrepreneur Logan Bisset finds solace in the arms of his ex, Quinn Murray. Meeting again at a Nantucket wedding, the heat's still there. But he might lose her again if he can't put the past behind him...

YOU CAN FIND MORE INFORMATION ON UPCOMING HARLEQUIN TITLES, FREE EXCERPTS AND MORE AT HARLEQUIN.COM.

HDCNM0122B

SPECIAL EXCERPT FROM

DESIRE

*Alaskan senator Jessup Outlaw needs an escape…
and he finds just what he needs on his Napa Valley
vacation: actress Paige Novak. What starts as a fling
soon gets serious, but a familiar face from Paige's past
may ruin everything…*

Read on for a sneak peek of
What Happens on Vacation…
by New York Times *bestselling author Brenda Jackson.*

"Hey, aren't you going to join me?" Paige asked, pushing wet hair back from her face and treading water in the center of the pool. "Swimming is on my list of fun things. We might as well kick things off with a bang."

Bang? Why had she said that? Lust immediately took over his senses. Desire beyond madness consumed him. He was determined that by the time they parted ways at the end of the month their sexual needs, wants and desires would be fulfilled and under control.

Quickly removing his shirt, Jess's hands went to his zipper, inched it down and slid the pants, along with his briefs, down his legs. He knew Paige was watching him and he was glad that he was the man she wanted.

"Come here, Paige."

She smiled and shook her head. "If you want me, Jess, you have to come and get me." She then swam to the far end of the pool, away from him.

Oh, so now she wanted to play hard to get? He had no problem going after her. Maybe now was a good time to tell her that not only had he been captain of his dog sled team, but he'd also been captain of his college swim team.

He glided through the water like an Olympic swimmer going after the gold, and it didn't take long to reach her. When she saw him getting close, she laughed and swam to the other side. Without missing a stroke or losing speed, he did a freestyle flip turn and reached out and caught her by the ankles. The capture was swift and the minute he touched her, more desire rammed through him to the point where water couldn't cool him down.

"I got you," he said, pulling her toward him and swimming with her in his arms to the edge of the pool.

When they reached the shallow end, he allowed her to stand, and the minute her feet touched the bottom she circled her arms around his neck. "No, Jess, I got you and I'm ready for you." Then she leaned in and took his mouth.

Don't miss what happens next in...
What Happens on Vacation...
by Brenda Jackson, the next book in her
Westmoreland Legacy: The Outlaws series!

Available March 2022 wherever
Harlequin Desire books and ebooks are sold.

Harlequin.com

Copyright © 2022 by Brenda Streater Jackson
HDEXP0122B

Get 4 FREE REWARDS!

We'll send you 2 FREE Books plus 2 FREE Mystery Gifts.

Harlequin Desire books transport you to the world of the American elite with juicy plot twists, delicious sensuality and intriguing scandal.

FREE
Value Over
$20

YES! Please send me 2 FREE Harlequin Desire novels and my 2 FREE gifts (gifts are worth about $10 retail). After receiving them, if I don't wish to receive any more books, I can return the shipping statement marked "cancel." If I don't cancel, I will receive 6 brand-new novels every month and be billed just $4.55 per book in the U.S. or $5.24 per book in Canada. That's a savings of at least 13% off the cover price! It's quite a bargain! Shipping and handling is just 50¢ per book in the U.S. and $1.25 per book in Canada.* I understand that accepting the 2 free books and gifts places me under no obligation to buy anything. I can always return a shipment and cancel at any time. The free books and gifts are mine to keep no matter what I decide.

225/326 HDN GNND

Name (please print)

Address   Apt. #

City   State/Province   Zip/Postal Code

Email: Please check this box ☐ if you would like to receive newsletters and promotional emails from Harlequin Enterprises ULC and its affiliates. You can unsubscribe anytime.

Mail to the Harlequin Reader Service:
IN U.S.A.: P.O. Box 1341, Buffalo, NY 14240-8531
IN CANADA: P.O. Box 603, Fort Erie, Ontario L2A 5X3

Want to try 2 free books from another series! Call 1-800-873-8635 or visit www.ReaderService.com.

---

*Terms and prices subject to change without notice. Prices do not include sales taxes, which will be charged (if applicable) based on your state or country of residence. Canadian residents will be charged applicable taxes. Offer not valid in Quebec. This offer is limited to one order per household. Books received may not be as shown. Not valid for current subscribers to Harlequin Desire books. All orders subject to approval. Credit or debit balances in a customer's account(s) may be offset by any other outstanding balance owed by or to the customer. Please allow 4 to 6 weeks for delivery. Offer available while quantities last.

Your Privacy—Your information is being collected by Harlequin Enterprises ULC, operating as Harlequin Reader Service. For a complete summary of the information we collect, how we use this information and to whom it is disclosed, please visit our privacy notice located at corporate.harlequin.com/privacy-notice. From time to time we may also exchange your personal information with reputable third parties. If you wish to opt out of this sharing of your personal information, please visit readerservice.com/consumerschoice or call 1-800-873-8635. **Notice to California Residents**—Under California law, you have specific rights to control and access your data. For more information on these rights and how to exercise them, visit corporate.harlequin.com/california-privacy.

HD21R2

**IF YOU ENJOYED THIS BOOK
WE THINK YOU WILL ALSO LOVE**

HARLEQUIN
ROMANTIC SUSPENSE

Danger. Passion. Drama.

These heart-racing page-turners will keep you guessing to the very end. Experience the thrill of unexpected plot twists and irresistible chemistry.

4 NEW BOOKS AVAILABLE EVERY MONTH!

HRSXSERIES2020

SPECIAL EXCERPT FROM

(H) HARLEQUIN
ROMANTIC SUSPENSE

*Interim police chief Marcus Price is captivated by
newcomer Erin McGarry, who has come to Knoware
to help her sick sister. But he has his hands full with a
string of robberies and a credible terrorist threat, and
he's not confident that Erin didn't bring the danger to
the small community or that either one of them will
survive it.*

Read on for a sneak preview of
Trouble in Blue,
*the next thrilling romance in Beverly Long's
Heroes of the Pacific Northwest series!*

Marcus watched as she got to her feet. He was grateful to
see that she was steady.

"Can we have a minute?" Marcus asked Blade.

"Yeah. Hang on to her good arm," his friend replied.
Then he walked away, taking Dawson with him.

"What?" she asked, offering him a sweet smile.

"I'm going to find who did this. I promise you. And
you're going to be okay. Jamie Weathers is the best
emergency physician this side of the Colorado River.
Hell, this side of the Missouri River. He'll fix you up.
But don't leave the hospital until you hear from me. You
understand?"

"I got it," she said. "I'm going to be fine. It's all going to be fine. I barely had twenty bucks in my bag. He didn't even get my phone. I had that in my back pocket. Nor my keys. Those were in my hand. So he basically got nothing except the cash and my driver's license."

Things didn't matter. "You want me to let Brian and Morgan know?"

"Oh, God, no. Please don't do that." She looked panicked. "Morgan can't have stress right now. I'm grateful that her room is on the other side of the building. Otherwise, she could be watching this spectacle."

They would want to know. But it was her decision. And she was in pain. "Okay," he said, giving in easily.

"Thank you," she said.

"Go get fixed up. I'll talk to you soon."

She nodded.

"And, Erin…" he added.

"Yeah."

"I'm really glad that you're okay."

Don't miss
Trouble in Blue *by Beverly Long,*
available March 2022 wherever
Harlequin Romantic Suspense
books and ebooks are sold.

Harlequin.com

CARROLL COUNTY

JAN 2022

PUBLIC LIBRARY

Copyright © 2022 by Beverly R. Long

HRSEXP0122B